# Table of Contents

# Introduction

This book will be structured using a historical approach and sociological perspective. It is important that the reader does not give up his or her point of view in an effort to understand the text. It is better to examine the text using one's own insight to better understand why individuals' views on the American justice system can differ to such a wide degree. A Black man coming of age in the 1960's and 1970's living in Rochester, New York would most likely have a different perspective than a White female millennial from the south. To better understand history, we must better understand each other. By sharing authentic perspectives, we will be able to generate respect and honest communication. Communication can affect change to better the institutions that run the United States of America.

T.W.I.C.E. (The World Is Changing Everyone)

This book examines three pillars upon which rest the American justice system. Law enforcement agencies and officers, along with courts, with a heavy emphasis on those which address criminal behavior. Last but not least of the three will be prisons and jails.

As a child in elementary school during the 1960s, I felt so very proud when I had learned to recite the Pledge of Allegiance. Every morning my classmates and I started our class day by reciting the pledge. Even living in a redlined neighborhood, policed by officers who treated those around me with contempt, was not enough to open my young eyes to the hypocrisy of that last sentence of the pledge. "With liberty and justice for all". Growing up in the 60's and 70's, I was a firsthand observer of the Civil Rights Movement. One of the goals of the movement was to help the country reach a stage whereby the words "liberty and justice for all" would become a reality.

As detailed in the first book of this series, Black America: A Broken Social Contract (J. Jones, 2020), the government in many instances, using the American justice system, crushed the movement before many of its goals could be realized. The COINTELPRO project initiated by the FBI under J. Edgar Hoover, operated with ruthless efficacy to murder and jail some leaders while destroying the characters of others. Being left leaderless meant that many poor Americans were akin to a rudderless ship in a storm.

The picture of Dr. King and the Kennedy brothers was very common in many Black households during the civil rights era. My mother had one prominently displayed in our dining room. The portrait piqued my curiosity to the point that one day I asked her about the importance of these men and why was this picture so widely circulated. Her reaction surprised me. She was in the process of cooking and washing clothes, yet she told me to sit down, and she sat with me. She probed my understanding of what I felt were the attributes of a good person. After I completed my explanation, she explained to me how these men had given their lives to help all Americans live their lives with freedom and equality. She went on to explain how some people in this country would not accept the change that would result if the words of Dr. King were to become a reality. Specifically, when he asked that all people not be judged by the color of their skin but by the content of their character.

George Orwell's book, 1984, was written in 1949. As our country moves closer to authoritarian rule, Orwellian views help one better understand how we arrived where we are and how we should move forward. Orwell stated that "who controls the past controls the future: who controls the present controls the past." Citizens of this country have been led to believe certain things about our justice system which are patently false. We must educate ourselves and take control of the present so as to restructure the justice system to ensure a better future institution dedicated to serving the people. Justice is not just unless everyone receives it.

# Introduction

# Chapter 1

# Origins of Policing

The founding fathers when writing the constitution were heavily influenced by enlightenment thinkers and philosophers. Men such as John Locke, Thomas Hobbs, and Jean Jacques Rousseau. These enlightenment luminaries were instrumental in introducing ideas that would move nations from the rule of monarchs to the governments that we see today.

A democratic government is heavily reliant upon the theories of enlightenment thinkers if it is truly designed to serve all citizens equally. American law should be derived from the constitution with its precepts of enlightenment philosophy. However, this has not always been the case. This deviation from the root principles of law is one reason why the American justice system in many cases is not just. One of the most important constructs of the enlightenment thinkers is the "Social Contract". Our constitution was created as a social contract for the country. A social contract can be described as an agreement, between the ruled and their rulers, defining the rights and duties of each. For the social contract to work, individuals must agree to forfeit some of their rights in exchange for protection and safety by the government. Starting from slaves and Native Americans being forcibly removed from their homes and murdered with no government protection, to Wounded Knee and COINTELPRO, has resulted in today's violence visited upon Freddie Gray, Sandra Bland and hundreds of others. It has become clear that for some, in our society, the Social Contract does not apply. To best understand why the social contract between individuals and the justice system has fractured, one must understand the three branches of government, and the history of policing.

The Federal Government is composed of three distinct branches: legislative, executive, and judicial. The role and power of each branch is ordained by the U.S. Constitution in the Congress, the President, and the Federal courts, respectively. The legislative branch makes laws (Congress, comprised of the House of Representatives and Senate). The executive branch carries out laws (president, vice president, cabinet, and most federal agencies). The judicial branch evaluates laws (supreme court and other federal courts). A prima facie examination of the organization and powers of the three branches leads one to believe that the American justice system is wholly capable of ensuring safety and justice for all citizens. However, history has proven such is not the case. I submit to you that the problem stems from a desire to control citizens rather than serve them. In order to correct the problems within our justice system, the three branches must be involved in amending the behaviors of those sworn to defend the constitution. The institution of a true social contract is required to fix the broken legal system.

First, we will take a look at the history of how and why police forces were established in this country. Understanding the reasons for creating police forces, and analyzing how they were initially used when coupled with sociological theory, brings some clarity to the current broken social contract. The importance of looking at the history lies in the sociological theory of R.E. Park. His work in "Human Ecology" speaks to a social order formed by sharp ethnic differences. He speaks about the division of labor between the classes and how those differences create conflict. Interaction with the legal system is heavily influenced by both ethnic differences and class. Minorities, and those on the lower end of the socioeconomic spectrum tend to receive unequal treatment from the justice system. Park also examines the importance of assimilation. Most ethnic groups upon large scale immigration to the country were discriminated against and denied a true social contract until they were able to assimilate into the social structure. Some ethnic groups, mainly those of color to include Native Americans, Blacks, Latinos, and Asians, have not been able to fully assimilate in this country. It is not the fault of these peoples that they have not been able to assimilate. Physical differences which are readily identifiable is the main issue. After a generation or two, the Ethno-Europeans would lose old world accents and adopt new world customs. Those changes allowed for them to blend in and assimilate. However, for those with readily identified physical differences such as skin color, assimilation wouldn't be as easy.

As we all know, conflict often results in interaction with the police. Lack of assimilation provides an out-group that police often treat in a manner not consistent with a working social contract. The creation of police forces in America came about for very different reasons depending upon what region of the country they were formed. In the south, the primary duties of the first police forces formed consisted mainly of slave catching. Slaves had no rights; therefore, slave catchers had no social contract with this outgroup. The majority of whites in the south were poor farmers who were wary of running afoul of large plantation owners; this outgroup had no real social contract with those slave patrols. The plantation owners commissioned and controlled the slave patrols. The vast sums of money amassed by large plantations afforded the owners power that in some instances were unchallenged. It also created a social contract between slave owners and what amounted to their personal police forces. It was this social contract that allowed the plantation system to become so successful. One must realize that on the large plantations there were many more slaves than masters. The slave owners would use violence and the threat of violence by armed vigilantes to prevent the slaves from rebelling. The tactic was especially effective because laws prevented the slaves from owning weapons.

Operant conditioning as described in the "Willie Lynch" letter in the first book of this series, Black America: A Broken Social Contract, (Jones, 2020) was one cornerstone of slave subjugation, and laws put in place that stripped slaves of human rights was the other. It is small wonder that the descendants of the oppressed slaves would come to look at law enforcement with little trust. Operant conditioning as championed by B.F. Skinner is a method of shaping behavior that utilizes rewards and punishments to obtain a desired outcome. Through operant conditioning, an association is made between a behavior and a consequence whether negative or positive for that behavior. When applied correctly, it is a powerful force in not only shaping behavior but thought processes as well. Operant conditioning tends to start as a short-term behavior modification tool which in many instances can become self-perpetuating. One of the most powerful aspects of operant conditioning is the self-perpetuating nature of this construct. Many of the societal ills suffered by Black and Native Americans stems from operant conditioning designed to place them in a permanent underclass. Fred Hampton describes the results and his solution.

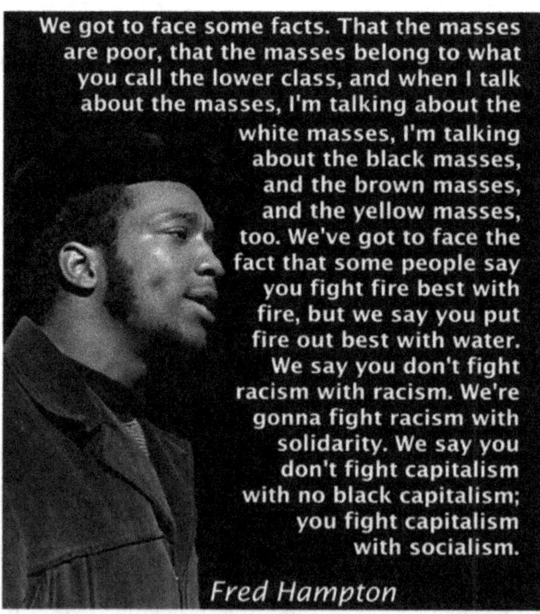


Policing in the north was a different paradigm when compared with the south. The first northern state to establish a professional police force was Massachusetts in the year 1838. By the late 1850's most major cities in the north operated a police force. New Orleans in the south, which was made up partly by a large urban area, had established a law enforcement agency more akin to its northern counterparts rather than its southern neighbors. The rapid population growth in urban areas spurred by the industrial revolution would manifest issues in the north that were not present in the south. The agrarian south did not have the level of problems endemic to urban areas. Burglary, assault, prostitution and a myriad of challenges encountered when large numbers of people are forced to live in close quarters gave the northern police a very different mission from their southern counterparts.

The early police forces in the north were established during the Gilded Age. This was a time in American history when 24 robber barons controlled most of the country. With their obscene wealth, they controlled politicians, judges, and the police. People hear names such as Rockefeller, Vanderbilt, Carnegie, and think of self-made men who helped America become a prosperous nation. This is a fallacy. Those robber barons were businessmen in the 19th century who engaged in unethical and monopolistic practices. They were often aided by corrupt politicians whom they controlled. In turn, those corrupt politicians controlled the police. These men faced almost no business regulation, and amassed enormous material wealth while most Americans struggled for survival. Robber barons and their families were kept safe. They were served by the political system and law enforcement. Robber barons and many other leaders during the Gilded Age kept order by using Machiavellian principles. The renaissance man, Machiavelli, "believed that, for a ruler, it was better to be widely feared than to be greatly loved; a loved ruler retains authority by obligation, while a feared leader rules by fear of punishment." As inequality widened during the Industrial Revolution, Machiavelli's principles held true. Not until the growth of labor unions during the latter part of the Gilded Age would the common man be able to gain some concessions from the wealthy. Sadly, the changes for the better would not apply to most minorities.

Changes to law enforcement in the south came about due to the Civil War. By the end of the war, slavery had been abolished leaving no need for slave catchers. America transitioned into a period called Reconstruction. The Reconstruction era was about a twelve-year period after the war, during which the United States navigated the challenges of reintegrating the states that had seceded into the Union. Among one of the greatest questions to be answered would be determining the legal status of African Americans.

Erin Blakemore's History & Culture Race in America (2021 explains:

"Tragedy reshaped the trajectory of Reconstruction—and ultimately undermined its promise. On April 15, 1865—just days after his final speech—Lincoln was assassinated and his vice president, Andrew Johnson, became president.

Although Johnson was a southern Democrat and a _former enslaver_ who had joined Lincoln on a unity ticket, most Republicans expected him to continue Lincoln's agenda. They underestimated Johnson's racism and southern sympathies. Johnson's vision for Reconstruction included blanket _pardons_ for most former Confederates, including many high-level officials, and a lenient stance toward rebel states. He made no attempt to integrate Black people into southern institutions" (Blakemore, 2021).

With a racist president such as Johnson, Reconstruction was doomed and those southern states that depended on slave labor to enrich the elites of their society would quickly take advantage.

From 1865 to 1866, Mississippi would set an example which was soon followed by all southern states. The legislature would enact Black Codes designed to restrict movement of newly freed African Americans and force them to work for little or no compensation. Peder Punsalan-Teigen, Blackpast writer (2021), describes Black Codes of the south :

"Under new apprenticeship laws, county law enforcement and civil officials were required to report all free minors of Black or mixed race, who were orphans, or whose parents were unable to provide financial care for them, to the courts. The courts could then order the minors to work as apprentices for individuals whom the courts deemed suitable and competent; however, a minor's former master had preference. In effect, this provision guaranteed that former owners had preference to ensure that the children of their former slaves would continue to labor for the master. Similarly, in the vagrancy provisions of the Black Codes, the Mississippi legislature stated that any freedman who was unemployed within two weeks of the new year in 1866, was a vagrant. A vagrant needed to pay a fine, and if the vagrant was unable to pay the fine within five days, then the vagrant would be forced into jail and ultimately into unpaid labor" (para. 5-6).

In an effort to maintain profits after the Civil War, the big landholders who once owned slaves would have to find a way to obtain cheap labor. The black codes would be codified into law and those laws would come to be known as Jim Crow laws. The Jim Crow laws would be enforced by local law enforcement, and soon promised a steady supply of labor to maximize the profits of former slaveholders once again.

Many former slaves and poor white farmers were duped into a system of permanent servitude. This was done through what is known as sharecropping. Sharecroppers were given a parcel of land to grow crops with the promise that all profits made from those crops would be divided between the lien holder and the sharecropper. There were also inferences made that the farmer would be able to purchase the land with future profits. Sharecropping was organized in such a fashion that the sharecropper would first pay the land holder with his share of the crops, and any crops left over for that season could be sold by the sharecropper who would then receive market value for the product. In reality, the system was designed to place the sharecropper in a debt cycle that could never be repaid. Therefore, the land would always remain with the land holder and could never be purchased by the sharecropper who would be in a perpetual state of debt. This debt cycle would start from the beginning of the contract, as the tenant farmers had no money to buy tools, seed, nor animals needed to make the farm work. They would obtain loans from the landowner at an exorbitant rate that could never be paid back by the meager earnings of the sharecropper. Since they had no cash, they were supplied with whatever they needed at a significant markup. Every season the sharecropper would fall deeper and deeper into debt with the land holder. Jim Crow laws dictated that no black person could leave the farm until all debts were paid by the sharecropper. This meant that not only was the sharecropper perpetually tied to the land but also his children. As black and white sharecroppers struggled to make the payments on their land in some instances, they would band together in an effort to gain better treatment. The white sharecroppers who tried to better their living situation by standing as a united front with the black sharecroppers would be ejected from their lands and ostracized by the community. The black farmers would be subject to incarceration to include working with the chain gang. This was all enforced by America's first homegrown terrorist organization, the local law-enforcement community.

The White supremacist group known as the Ku Klux Klan was originally organized in Tennessee as an organization for southern Civil War veterans and would soon become the right hand of Jim Crow in the south. One of its first leaders was a retired civil war General by the name of Nathan Bedford Forrest. They would become known not only as the Ku Klux Klan, but also night riders. They covered their faces with hoods and wore sheets to intimidate their victims. This mode of dress was not truly to disguise themselves, for they had no fear of being known. Many of the members were the elites of society in the south and also law-enforcement. During their stranglehold on the south, they would go on to murder, intimidate, mutilate, and instill fear in victims they desired to subjugate. This would go on from the end of the Civil War until 1968 when most Jim Crow laws were struck down. By1968, a concerted effort by the federal government to beat back the violence of the Klan would start to lessen its numbers and its impact. But the Klan would never truly die.

"Lynching were violent public acts that white people used to terrorize and control Black people in the 19th and 20th centuries, particularly in the South. Lynching typically evoke images of Black men and women hanging from trees, but they involved other extreme brutality, such as torture, mutilation, decapitation, and desecration. Some victims were burned alive" (NAACP, 2022, para. 2).

Between the years 1888 and 1968, the NAACP records over 4700 lynching's in the United States. Over 3400 of those people lynched were

Black Americans and a large number of non-blacks lynched were whites and people of other races who tried to help blacks or were anti-lynching.

One reason lynching came into vogue after the Civil War was because it was a very effective way to control black people who know longer were owned, and therefore had no monetary value to their former slave holders. Due to the high cost for a slave lynching during slavery, lynching was mitigated, as the slaveholder did not want to lose his or her money from their property being "destroyed." Once Blacks were no longer property, that was no longer the case. Lynching was one of the many tools used by the Ku Klux Klan and others who were intent on keeping the south as it was before the Civil War and the abolition of slavery.

Although most statistics for lynching's ended in 1968, there were still lynchings after that date. Many of those who were lynched were taken from jails without due process and murdered while whites watched and many reveled, as if it were a picnic or sporting event. There was no recourse for the families of those who were murdered often with the assistance of law enforcement. It amazes me that many politicians would like to erase this history by labeling it as Critical Race Theory (CRT) and claiming that white children should not have to learn this history because it will make them feel uncomfortable. In reality, CRT is a concept that is taught mostly at the post-secondary and graduate level.

As law-enforcement grew in the region, most southern cities did not have Black law enforcement officers until the mid-60s. I served for the Columbus, Georgia police department in the early 2000s. My first section Sergeant was one of the first Black officers to be hired in the Columbus Police Department. One day, he explained to me that the black police officers were only allowed to patrol in black neighborhoods. He also enlightened me to the fact that those black officers were not allowed to arrest white suspects. Please wrap your mind around the last sentence. The second largest city in the state of Georgia did not hire black officers until the mid-60s. Those officers did not have arrest powers for all citizens who committed crimes. They could only arrest black people whom they suspected of a crime. Individuals felt like equality was gained by the city hiring black officers. However, this is a paradigm that I cannot accept.

In the state of Mississippi, on June 12, 1963, the civil rights leader Medgar Evers was murdered by a White Supremacist named Byron De la Beckwith. This man would not be convicted of the murder by a jury of his peers. He was convicted of conspiracy to murder, and this occurred in 1977, 14 years after the crime. The first two cases concerning De la Beckwith would end up in hung juries in 1963 and 1964. Prior to his conviction, he was a free man who often bragged about what he had done until his conviction in 1977. This murderer served only three years in prison for his deeds and was paroled. His story is only one of many similar instances in which law enforcement failed in providing their service as part of the social contract.

Sundown towns are all-white communities in the United States that practice a form of racial segregation–excluding non-whites by using some combination of discriminatory local laws, intimidation or violence. Most individuals would think that in the year 2022, such a thing as sundown towns would not exist. Yet, they do, and are a clear and present danger to all minorities.

Ade Onibada (2021) writes "In 2017, the NAACP issued a <u>travel warning</u> for the entire state of Missouri– a first for the organization. The decision was in response to a <u>bill</u> designed to limit discrimination lawsuits by making changes to the Missouri Human Rights Act. <u>Senate Bill No. 43</u> would require employees prove that their protected characteristics were a "motivating factor" for being discriminated against, when previously, the requirement simply showed it was a "contributing factor"' (para. 9)

The NAACP also referenced anecdotal examples of hate crimes and data which showed Black motorists were <u>75% more likely</u> to be pulled over, stopped, and searched by police enforcement than their white counterparts. Notingly, the state of Missouri offered no public response to the NAACP, but did make a <u>Black woman the face of its tourism campaign</u> last year. The fact that Black motorists make contact with law enforcement at such a disproportionate rate is an indicator of either unconscious bias or racial profiling.

For those who say there is now a valid social contract in the country, please allow me to share these facts:

"A Reuters <u>investigation</u> on May 6 indicates that a significant number of U.S. police instructors have ties to a constellation of armed right-wing militias and white supremacist hate groups–a report that adds to a fast-growing body of evidence showing a deadly threat inside U.S. police departments" (Kanu, 2022, para. 1).

The investigation adds to mounting academic research, government audits and <u>news</u> <u>reporting</u> that demonstrates the pervasiveness of white supremacy in U.S. law enforcement, and a continuing series of incidents documenting the presence of extremist groups and views among law enforcement" (Kanu, 2022, para. 3).

The numbers from the study reported by Kanu (2022) were collected from law-enforcement agencies across the country, not just those in the south. The investigation reveals a very real threat to not just minorities but all Americans who might oppose the views of those white supremacist ideals.

Due to a different demographic and the absence of slavery, the evolution of law-enforcement in the north was very different from that of law-enforcement in the south. One thing they did have in common was a lack of a social contract for minorities and the poor.

At the inception of law-enforcement in the north, there was rampant corruption throughout government in most cities. The façade that most see and are taught about law-enforcement in the north is that by the 1960s, the majority of the force was professionally free of graft, and ready to protect and serve all. In reality, corruption and graft have never fully been eliminated in those departments. This is due mainly to a code of ethics whereby one officer will not testify against another who may have committed a crime. This is a part of the code that makes up the thin blue line. To cross this line would place the individual who does so in the status of an outcast, one who cannot be trusted by his fellow officers and therefore would lose the support of many of those officers. This lack of support would impact the officer's safety and ability to perform the job. To better illustrate this, we will discuss the case of Frank Serpico, a police officer who crossed the line, almost costing him his life, later on in this chapter.

The New York City Police Department was established in 1845. To better understand the NYPD in its infancy, one must understand the political climate of the time. Boss Tweed (William, M. Tweed) was a larger-than-life politician who was famous for his corruption and cronyism. Tammany Hall was the Democratic political machine through which Tweed embezzled vast amounts of money from the city of New York. Boss Tweed was elected to his first position as an alderman. He quickly moved up the ladder and gained control of the city's Democratic Party. To better control the government and shape it to fit his personal needs, he filled important positions with people friendly to his governance. As Katrina Schwartz (2020) states in her article about August Vollmer, the man credited for modern-day policing in the U.S.

"This was a moment in the history of American policing called the Political Era. Police were entirely beholden to whoever held political power. They did what the mayor told them, whether it was garnering good will by reuniting lost children with their parents, breaking up strikes or dragging people to the polls and telling them how to vote" (para. 9)

Any law enforcement officer during this time would find it necessary to focus on staying in the good graces of the bosses, rather than concentrating on police work. The low wages paid to police were supplemented by taking payoffs from criminals, and this would become a systemic problem throughout the department.

William DeLong (2021) writes, "Born Francesco Vincent Serpico into an Italian-American family, young Serpico idolized the NYPD cops who patrolled his neighborhood in the Bedford-Stuyvesant section of Brooklyn. Serpico consequently joined the New York police force in 1959 in a bid to follow in the footsteps of his childhood heroes. Serpico's spirit was slowly crushed as he witnessed the rampant corruption in his precinct. Cops were bribed by criminals, gamblers, thugs, and drug dealers with everything from free meals to money. His refusal to partake in these practices made Serpico all the more unpopular at his job" (para. 5)

Serpico complained to his superiors and even named individuals he knew of who were accepting bribes. No action was taken against the officers named. While on the job in Brooklyn, Serpico was shot in the face while participating in a drug raid in 1971; months before he was due to testify. It was Serpico's assertion that none of the officers with him called the shooting in as an officer down. Frank survived and later spoke in front of the Knapp Commission on police corruption. Below is an abstract of the Knapp Commissions findings in 1973.

## KNAPP COMMISSION REPORT
## ON POLICE CORRUPTION

**NCJ Number**

10579
**Author(s)**

ANON
**Date Published**

1973
**Length**

296 pages

THE COMMISSION FOUND CORRUPTION TO BE WIDESPREAD, ALTHOUGH BY NO MEANS UNIFORM IN DEGREE. CORRUPT POLICEMEN ARE DESCRIBED AS EITHER, 'GRASS-EATERS' WHO ACCEPT THE PAY-OFFS AND GRATUITIES THAT THE CIRCUMSTANCES OF POLICE WORK MAY DEVELOP, AND 'MEAT-EATERS', A SMALL

PERCENTAGE OF THE FORCE, WHO AGGRESSIVELY EXPLOIT SITUATIONS FOR LARGE PAYOFFS. CHAPTERS COVER THE DISTINCTIVE PATTERNS OF GAMBLING, NARCOTICS, PROSTITUTION, THE CONSTRUCTION INDUSTRY, AND OTHER ELEMENTS INVOLVING GRAFT AND CORRUPTION. THE REASON FOR PAYOFFS, METHODS USED, AND INTERRELATIONSHIPS OF CORRUPTION FACTORS ARE DISCUSSED IN DETAIL. THE TYPE OF GRAFT WHICH A CORRUPT POLICEMEN ACCEPTS IS DETERMINED BY HIS CHARACTER, THE DEPARTMENT TO WHICH HE IS ASSIGNED, THE GEOGRAPHIC AREA IN WHICH HE WORKS, AND HIS RANK AND SPECIFIC DUTIES. THE LARGEST SOURCES OF POLICE PAYOFFS ARE ORGANIZED CRIME AND LEGITIMATE BUSINESS. THE GREATEST OBSTACLE TO ANTICORRUPTION EFFORTS IS A FEELING OF GROUP LOYALTY IN THE POLICE FORCE WHICH GENERATES HOSTILITY TO ATTEMPTS TO EXPOSE CORRUPTION AND A CONCOMITANT CODE OF SILENCE. THE COMMISSION SUGGESTS AN INSPECTIONAL SERVICES BUREAU TO SPEARHEAD AN ALL-OUT ATTACK WHICH INCLUDE REDUCING THE OPPORTUNITIES AND TEMPTATIONS FOR CORRUPT ACTIVITY, INCREASING THE RISKS FOR GIVERS AND TAKERS OF BRIBES, AND CHANGING CERTAIN POLICE PROCEDURES TO REDUCE DEPARTMENT LIABILITY TO CORRUPTION.

Although the Knapp Commission was able to identify much of the corruption, it was not able to eliminate it. Over the years, best practices have done much to address systemic corruption, but due to the code of silence there are still officers committing criminal acts that violate a true social contract. To better understand the code of silence within law enforcement, it is necessary to recognize the groupthink phenomenon and its power to pressure individuals to ignore what is right to gain acceptance.

According to Kendra Cherry (2022), "Groupthink is a psychological phenomenon in which people strive for consensus within a group. In many cases, people will set aside their own personal beliefs or adopt the opinion of the rest of the group. The term was first used in 1972 by <u>social psychologist</u> Irving L. Janis.

People who are opposed to the decisions or overriding opinion of the group as a whole frequently remain quiet, preferring to keep the peace rather than disrupt the uniformity of the crowd. The phenomenon can become problematic, but even well-intentioned people are prone to making irrational decisions in the face of overwhelming pressure from the group" (para. 1 2).

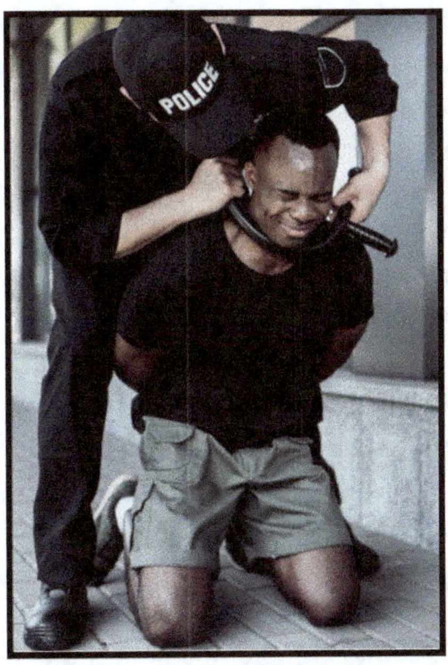


What is not taken into account in most incidents of police malfeasance is the lack of trust that these bad actors wearing badges create amongst hard-working law-abiding citizens; who will no longer trust the police.

Willard M. Oliver, a criminal justice professor in the Department of Criminal Justice at Sam Houston State University and author of <u>August Vollmer: The Father of American Policing</u> characterizes Vollmer as "one of the most extraordinary men ever elected town marshal and appointed police chief in American history. It was Vollmer who brought policing out of its wholly corrupt and often brutal era of politics, by professionalizing not only his own police department in Berkeley, California, but police departments across the country and around the world. He was instrumental in the creation of the polygraph machine (lie detector), patrol car radio communication systems, and, as the Los Angeles Police Chief, the first crime lab in America. His greatest legacy, however, was the higher education program he created at UC Berkeley, which developed into the disciplines of criminal justice and criminology that are so widespread today" (para. 1)

Much of the literature that chronicles the evolution of policing in America describes August Vollmer as the father of American policing. There is no argument from me that this is a true statement. And by accepting this truth, one must look further than the surface of his accomplishments. Not only was he the father of American law enforcement, but he was also a true believer in eugenics. His belief in eugenics included the paradigm that some races were not as developed as others. Eugenics teaches that the white race is superior to others in morals and intellect. One must ask, did his belief in eugenics help shape the methodology that he brought forth to modern policing? In observing the differential treatment of many police officers when interacting with minorities, the answer would be yes. We often see the over policing of minorities and a lack of respect given to those people by the police.

Individuals tend to confuse labels and catchphrases used to address unwanted behavior. One that is particularly misconceived is Black Lives Matter. The phrase does not mean that Black lives are more important than the lives of any other ethnic group or the police. It does mean that equality should be the norm for all races when law enforcement is involved. This presently is clearly not the case. In many instances, law enforcement interactions result in a broken social contract with many of those people whom the police are supposed to protect. This book could list dozens of names of unarmed black men and women who have been killed by the police. This has gone on since the advent of law enforcement. To this day, many believe that those minorities who were killed deserved what happened because they failed to obey law enforcement officers' commands. Now there are many of these incidents, since that of Rodney King, that are detailed in videos. The images and actions captured and shown allow those who did not believe police officers were capable of abusing their powers, to see the truth with their own eyes.

Please understand, I do not advocate for the elimination of the police. To do so would create a feudal society and ensure that life is "nasty brutish and short." I am not of the mindset that defunding the police would be a positive. It breaks my heart that those great officers who believe in their oath and risk their lives every day to protect us, also carry the stain created by colleagues who cannot be trusted with a potato gun.

The evolution of policing is riddled with many sociological theories. The sociological work known as "Sociocultural Evolution" is one that is central in understanding the growth of law enforcement in America. The sociologist, Gerhard Lenski, states: "Societal survival has been largely a function of a society's level of technological advance relative to the societies with which it has been in competition".

Gerhard Lenski developed an approach to studying sociology that is very different from that of many sociologists. His method of examining society and social structure stresses a focus on the social and cultural elements of society while providing an evolutionary perspective. Lenski's work involves macrosociology, which is the study of society as a whole. He views human society from the lens of change tied to society's level of innovation. His paradigm for this course of development is Sociocultural Evolution. His work provides hope for those of us who see a changing landscape in America. The cross section of societal demographics that participated in protest after the murder of George Floyd demonstrated how many individuals understand the need for change in law enforcement procedures. Yet, it may not happen as quickly as many feel it should. Change will come as long as the majority of people demand it.

We understand the systemic problems in policing and the solutions. In the next chapter I will speak to the pros and cons of the current system. I will also put forth fixes to move policing to another level and repair the broken social contract.

# Chapter 2

# **Pros and Cons of Policing**

The evolution of policing does not paint a very good portrait of law enforcement. The facts were provided to help the reader understand why there is so much mistrust between minorities and the police. Please understand that the previous chapter was not designed to denigrate the police; it was written to help the reader understand how we arrived at where we are today. As a former officer, I have friends who are still with the police force. To Chris, Tim, Ivan, Allan, and all of the officers who put on that uniform and uphold their oath of office every day, I would like to say I love and respect you. It is your hard work and dedication that gives me hope that this broken social contract can be repaired.

As the older officers who came along during a time when the system was inundated with prejudice and racism depart, the window has begun to open, giving space to throw out the old ways. While some departments fail to meet the bar as a whole–especially in large urban areas when it comes to treatment of all demographics, many are attempting to implement community policing and other programs that encourage positive community interactions. Some law enforcement agencies realize that it is time for a transition in order to meet the requirements necessary for a valid social contract to be a reality.

This chapter will focus on strengths, opportunities, weaknesses, and threats endemic to the current institution of public safety. Measures to correct problems will be infused throughout this section.

| Strengths<br>Military Structure<br>Equipment<br>State Certification | Weaknesses<br>Professional Development<br>Poor Pay Scale<br>Distrust in the Community<br>White Supremacy |
|---|---|
| Opportunities<br>Integrate Soft Skills<br>Link Advancement to Performance<br>Change Community Perception | Threats<br>Resistance to Change<br>Infiltration of Domestic Terrorist<br>Loss of Respect |

In chapter one, the paradigm of groupthink was discussed to help the reader understand why it is so difficult to cross the thin blue line even when an individuals' ethics and morals tell them it is the right thing to do. Groupthink is one weakness. A second weakness is unconscious bias. Unconscious biases are simply social stereotypes and tropes about certain groups of people that individuals form outside their own conscious awareness. The results can be horrific when they negatively affect an individual who holds as much power as a police officer. Examples of its effects on U.S citizens are heartbreaking and reinforce the beliefs that some lives are valued more than others.

Such was the case in the mass shooting at New York supermarket where a gunman in military-style clothing "opened fire with a rifle at a supermarket in Buffalo, killing 10 people and wounding three others in what authorities called a 'hate crime and racially motivated violent extremism,'" before being taken into custody Saturday afternoon, law enforcement officials said" (Collins et al., 2022, para. 1).

Collins et al, (2022) further describes what witnesses recounted, "'He was standing there with the gun to his chin. We were like what the heck is going on? Why does this kid have a gun to his face?' Kephart said. He dropped to his knees. 'He ripped off his helmet, dropped his gun, and was tackled by the police.' The shooter was apprehended without incident"' (para. 20)

Here is a case where the suspect had killed a former police officer and nine others. The police confronted an armed, active shooter, yet they displayed enough empathy to allow him to surrender without police firing one shot.

The White gunman's treatment by police officers when juxtaposed with officer's treatment of Black people accused of breaking the law reveal a glaring disparity. Take the case of Jayland Walker who Emma Tucker (2022) reports alleged misconduct in the police department's handling of Walker after a high-speed chase: "The decision by Ohio police officers to handcuff Jayland Walker after they fired dozens of shots, killing the unarmed 25-year-old at the end of a high-speed chase, has come under intense scrutiny by Walker's family and the public, as they continue to demand answers and accountability from city officials" (para. 3).

Walker, who suffered more than 60 gunshot wounds after eight officers fired at him June 27th, 2022 in Akron, "had his hands cuffed behind his back when his body arrived at the coroner's office, according to photos from a preliminary medical examiner's report reviewed by CNN. He died from gunshot wounds to the face, abdomen and upper legs, CNN affiliate NEWS reported, citing an investigative worksheet reviewed by its partner, the Akron Beacon Journal" ((Sandoval & Couwels, 2022, para. 1-2).

**Police violence in minority communities have led to recent calls for justice via a resurgence of civil disobedience and calls for government intervention.**

The two incidents described above illustrate why minorities have so much distrust for the police. In the first article, the shooter that killed 10 people in Buffalo, New York was a young white male. Those who have a working knowledge of how the police operate understand that when they are dispatched to a scene, the dispatcher describes the situation that they are going to encounter. So those officers knew that there was an armed white active shooter firing upon civilians in the supermarket. When they encountered this armed individual, their first instinct was not to fire and eliminate the threat. Instead, they chose to watch in curiosity as he brandished a weapon. Any movement by an individual who has just shot and killed 10 people, including a retired police officer, should trigger a response by officers on the scene. Yet, they allowed the shooter to transition from a standing to a kneeling position, still maintaining control of his weapon, which meant he could have fired on them at any second. Once again there was no response as far as discharging weapons by the police.

In the case of the second article, the black male motorist who was shot 60 times was unarmed and running away. Despite running away, which is not a threat posture, eight police officers fired upon this man accused of a traffic violation. Sixty shots hit the unarmed black teen who was cuffed with his hands behind his back, instead of receiving medical aid. Was it unconscious bias that led to the two very different approaches to these individuals? Was it unconscious bias that led these officers to believe a man who was fleeing away from them and unarmed was dangerous enough to shoot 60 times, while the white suspect who was armed in front of them "posed no threat?"

Recognizing unconscious bias in oneself is a very difficult proposition. Understanding that negative bias may be present in one's operating schema is the first step in overcoming the bias. There are some proven traits that will help to mitigate unconscious bias. They are called soft skills. Soft skills must be emphasized in any police training and evaluation program if it is to be successful in a holistic mode. There are some key personality traits that the military focuses on when evaluating soldiers for leadership and effectiveness. Those same personality traits would also prepare officers in law enforcement to become better public servants by strengthening soft skills and eliminating much officer stress. A list of personality traits includes: 1. Integrity 2. Adaptability 3. Communication Skills 4. Compassion 5. Conflict-Resolution 6. Initiative 7. Conscientiousness 8. Problem Solving 9. Ethics.

One strength of most police forces is the similarity to military structure. As an infantry soldier with 22 years of experience, I will argue that we have the best military in the world. The nine traits or soft skills listed above is one reason why. For a soldier to become an NCO and leader of men and women, he or she must grow these traits and display them in their daily interactions.

The army has designed an evaluation process, which is structured to identify strengths and weaknesses to superiors and subordinate individuals. A similar paradigm could be adopted by the police for officer development. It must be constructed in such a way to allow for and encourage growth of the individual. The strategy would involve three formative assessments, which consist of the leader and subordinate reviewing performance together during each quarter. A summative assessment would be finalized at the end of the fourth quarter. All deficiencies should be addressed and corrected before the summative assessment is administered. Any officer who has not corrected problem areas after year one should receive remedial training. Those individuals who still have issues after year two should receive a pay freeze with no advancement in rank until all problem areas are up to standard. Any officer failing to meet the standards by year three should be considered for termination.

There is an old adage that says you get what you pay for. In a follow-up story to the police shooting of Michael Brown, NBC News reporters (2014) found that, "police officers throughout St. Louis County were dispatched there to respond to mounting protests. Though the officers were doing the same jobs, they were paid starkly different wages, some as low as $10.50 an hour.

Data obtained by NBC News from 24 municipal police departments in St. Louis County reveal a gulf between police officer pay in poor, majority African American northern cities and wealthier, whiter cities further south. Average annual patrol officer pays ranges from $23,000 in Hillsdale to nearly $70,000 in Town and County and Des Peres" (para. 1-2)

It befuddles me that we ask men and women to put their lives on the line every day to protect ours, yet we do not compensate them fairly. There are many officers around the country with families who qualify for public assistance. This encourages situations in which officers work multiple outside jobs to survive. Some of these men and women do not receive enough rest and time for their bodies and minds to stay healthy. The department in which I worked operated with six days on and three days off for officers assigned to patrol. It was common for some officers to work sixty days or more without a day off. This, for many with children, was out of necessity.

An easy fix for pay issues would be to link starting pay to the average median income of the area in which the officer works. To ensure compression pay issues do not occur, use a benchmark such as the Consumer Price Index. Ensure that officers' salaries are correlated with the CPI. As the CPI rises, so would pay. Once officer pay has become a livable wage, external part time jobs can be regulated by departments to ensure officers are always ready for their primary duties.

One of the more insidious issues plaguing police departments involves the infiltration of White supremacists. The holy trinity that White supremacists are looking to infect and recruit from are law enforcement, the military, and first responders. This matter has become so acute that the federal government has passed laws and directed resources to counter the White supremacist agenda.

Listed below is the heading of a congressional subcommittee hearing headed by U.S. Representative Jamie Raskin of Maryland (Confronting Violent White Supremacy Part IV: White Supremacy in Blue_The Infiltration of Local Police Departments, 2020)

**CONFRONTING VIOLENT WHITE SUPREMACY**
**(PART IV): WHITE SUPREMACY IN BLUE— THE**
**INFILTRATION OF LOCAL POLICE DEPARTMENTS**
**Tuesday, September 29, 2020**
HOUSE OF REPRESENTATIVES SUBCOMMITTEE ON
CIVIL RIGHTS AND CIVIL LIBERTIES
COMMITTEE ON OVERSIGHT AND REFORM
*Washington, D.C.*

The paragraph below illustrates some of the contents of the document.

*"Mr. RASKIN. This is the fourth hearing our subcommittee has had on the problem of White supremacist violence in America. Since the murders of George Floyd and Breonna Taylor, we have also held a separate set of briefings on police brutality in communities of color and rampant violations of the First Amendment at civil rights protests by the Trump administration"* (Confronting Violent White Supremacy Part IV: White Supremacy in Blue_The Infiltration of Local Police Departments, 2020, para. 9)

We'll examine how these different threats to the American people intersect. Namely, how White supremacist organizations, ideas, and attitudes have come to infiltrate and target certain domains of law enforcement."

The most powerful train on the tracks causing these people to act out is the White Replacement Theory. This theory states that welcoming immigration ideals, especially those impacting non white immigrants, are part of a conspiracy designed to undermine or supersede the political power and culture of white people in countries like the U.S. Many forms of this conspiracy theory have been and continue to be used by anti-immigrant groups and White supremacists. Some politicians and White supremacists often use a three-point attack to spread their vitriol. ***Step one***: use of violent rhetoric of a migrant invasion. ***Step two:*** profess that non white immigrants will vote a certain way, and therefore pro-immigration policies are designed by elites to diminish the political influence of white Americans. ***Step three:*** employ the insidious practice of antisemitism.

People who subscribe to this conspiracy theory falsely claim that Jewish elites are responsible for the ***replacement*** efforts. This led to the violent protest in Charlottesville in which marchers chanted, "Jews Will Not Replace Us." Over the past 10 years, Anti-Semitic violence has increased exponentially. Much of it is due to this flawed replacement conspiracy.

For me, it was difficult to believe that people could be programmed to take the replacement theory as true. I watched nothing but right-wing news sites for four weeks. I didn't look for information on social media platforms, nor did I watch any news stations that might offer information counter to the narratives of the target stations. I've come to realize that because politicians, among others, come on these sites and support nonsense, it is easy to understand how some take these conspiracy theories as gospel. As a country, if we are to promote truth and respect there must be an effort to differentiate fake news and commentary from what is real.

Another problem that must be addressed is ridding the system of bad actors who use the badge in furthering criminal behavior.

Dana Goodyear, (2022) writes in The New Yorker, "According to a lawsuit filed by eight East L.A. deputies and the A.C.L.U., the Banditos gang 'controls the East Los Angeles station like inmates running a prison yard.' Leaders, known as 'shot callers,' determined deputies' hours, promotions, even days off. On patrol, they operated in the gray areas of law enforcement. Deputy Gonzalez said that they perpetuated 'the code of silence, the culture of the ghetto gunslinger.' She added, "What makes East L.A. so unique is it's embedded within the Hispanic machismo culture and the Hispanic street gangs" (para.5).

The mark of a Bandito, [or Mexican bandit,] is a secret numbered tattoo: a skeleton wearing a thick mustache, a bandolier, and a sombrero, and brandishing a smoking gun. (Deputy-gang tattoos are typically on the leg or the ankle.) Families of those killed by deputies allege that the deputies were "chasing ink"— trying to earn a tattoo. In a recent exposé on CBS News, anonymous whistle-blowers at East L.A. Station said, "If you get in a shooting, that's a definite brownie point [with the Banditos]" para. 5-6)

How can the folks in those areas, controlled by criminal sheriff's deputies, feel safe? There is no social contract when those we entrust to provide safety for us exhibit such behavior. The actions of these individuals tarnish the badge and all those who wear it.

In order to address criminal behavior by law enforcement, we need professional civilian review boards. Rather than boards being established and manned by community activists who may have personal vendettas, the boards should consist of federal employees with no ties to the department. These boards should have subpoena power and the ability to call a grand jury. No more police investigating their own. Last, but not least, qualified immunity should be terminated for all law enforcement offices. As it stands when officers violate citizens' rights, the money paid in settlements is taxpayer dollars. If officers had to worry about lawsuits utilizing their personal funds, many would reconsider abusing their power.

Listed in this chapter are strengths, weaknesses, opportunities, and threats involving law enforcement. There are a myriad of issues not spoken to, as to list them all would make this book longer than the bible. Additionally, the fixes provided are not the only tools in the toolbox to take care of the problems listed. There is always more than one way to skin a cat.

Most people would not use scissors to shave or a hammer to kill a fly. The proper tool for the proper job is always best. As institutions and people operate differently depending on regional mores, local issues should always be a priority when shaping services for the public.

Often, police officers are used for the wrong tasks. When most police departments are short on personnel, resources must be used wisely. Because officers are responsible for enforcing traffic codes, does not mean they should be the primary entity to resolve accidents. It would not be difficult to hire and train civilians as accident reconstruction specialists, thereby freeing up law enforcement for more police-oriented duties.

Juvenile offenders should not come in contact with traditional law enforcement, unless an offense was previously made regarding one of the three–robbery, rape, or murder. Juveniles would best be served by being introduced to an environment that is able to service their emotional and educational needs, while correcting the undesired behavior. An environment that prepares them to be law abiding citizens who contribute to the community rather than those who take from it while on the road to incarceration. The country must find a way to take some items off of the plates of the police so they can focus on public safety.

The laws of physics dictate that for every action, there is an opposite and equal reaction. The same paradigm holds true for sociology. The study of sociology involves the methodology of examining various established theories. While some sociologists believe in and use ideas such as ***Social Darwinism*** to form and guide their work, others prefer more inclusive approaches that consider macro-sociology, utilizing a much broader approach in the quest for truth.

One of my favorite old school sociologists is Talcottt Parsons. Parsons was one of the first to introduce social control to sociology. His theory continues to be a vital instrument in understanding not only the importance of social control, but it also speaks to its methods. While the threat of punishment is only one tool, it is the primary method used when it pertains to law enforcement. His thesis maintains that gaining cooperation in a society is not only obtained by external agencies coercing individuals to obey rules through the threat of punishment, but through individuals internalizing norms and values through socialization.

*It is a lack of positive socialization that contributes so mightily in the school to prison pipeline.*

The mores and norms of most children in poverty tend to be very different from the mainstream, as influenced by the subset of culture in which they live. Thus, one of the more important actions vs. reactions in society requires the research and analysis of the instruments of control in a society. These control measures are designed to provide tools which ensure that individuals recognize and respect those norms which maintain social order and cohesion. In order to improve relations between law enforcement and citizens, officers must realize that serving the public and dispensing social control are not mutually exclusive. In reality, if trust and cooperation are to be attained, it is imperative that officers recognize the symbiotic relationship between the two concepts.

# Chapter 3

# The Courts

The Judiciary Act of 1789 is known as An Act to Establish the Judicial Courts of the United States. The bill was signed into law by President George Washington on September 24, 1789. Article III of the Constitution established a Supreme Court, but left Congress the authority to create lower federal courts as needed.

While researching this topic, I came across a site titled, *Origins and Foundations of American Courts*. The site correctly states that, "The Sixth

Amendment in the Bill of Rights guarantees, among other ideas, speedy and public trials, that defendants shall be informed of all charges against them, and a trial by jury. The idea of juries is so closely interwoven with that of the courts, that for most members of the American public, the image of a courtroom means a judge in a black robe, the persuasive legal advocate and the rows of twelve men and women looking on and listening closely to the testimony as it unfolds. Although the United States accounts for 90% of the jury trials held throughout the world today, most of the work conducted in a typical American court takes place without a jury" (para. 3.

The sheer numbers of defendants overwhelm the court system, and results in individuals charged with a crime, who may be innocent, suffering the effects of incarceration. Let's look at the process. When one has been charged with a crime, the first step in the criminal procedure is an arraignment.

During this first step, the individual appears before a judge in a courtroom. The procedure involves you being read the crime you've been charged with and entering your initial plea of guilty, not guilty, or no contest. Then comes the second phase of the American justice system in court, whereby money comes into play. Individuals who can afford it have already hired a lawyer. The lawyer has advised their clients of everything that will occur, depending on the suspects plea. It is at this point that the defendant makes a plea of guilty, not guilty, or no contest. If he or she pleads not guilty the lawyer, then argues for the lowest bail possible. Most judges will then set bail at a reasonable amount, enough to ensure the defendant shows up for trial. Those who cannot afford an attorney are assigned an overworked public defender who does not have the time or resources to represent his client in the same manner as a private attorney. The cruelest blow of all is that those individuals who cannot hire a private attorney, in most instances, cannot afford bail. These defendants are now incarcerated to await trial in a detention facility. Some suspects spend months and even years waiting for their case. In the meantime, jobs are lost, families are evicted, and individuals have no resources to prepare a defense to refute the charges levied against them. Last, but most insidious, is the fact that these people are now housed with convicted criminals and treated as such.

Atoosa Moinzadeh (2017), for Fader writes, "In 2010, then-16-year-old Kalief Browder was stopped by police on the way home from a party in the Belmont section of the Bronx. Accused of stealing a backpack, Browder ended up at Rikers Island, consequently losing three years of his life to the system for a crime he didn't commit.

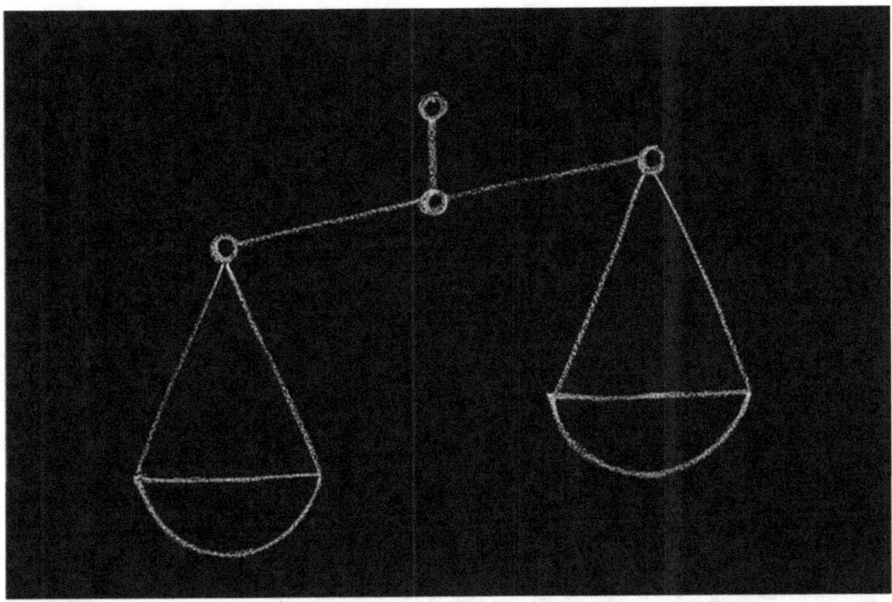

Deeply impacted by the trauma of his time at Rikers, Browder took his own life in 2015. His mother, Venida Browder, passed away shortly after. This story caught the attention of The Cinemart agency, Harvey Weinstein, and Jay Z, who partnered for the production of a six-part documentary series: TIME: The Kalief Browder Story, which airs on Netflix. Director Jenner Furst told The FADER that the partnership's hope was to make the series "one of the biggest stories of criminal justice there is, and to make sure Kalief Browder's name never disappears, that it lives forever" (para. 1-2).

Browder was a child. Just 16 years old when he was detained at New York City's Rikers Island jail on theft charges. Browder spent a total of two years in solitary confinement during his incarceration.

There is video of the youngster being beaten by a guard and jumped by inmates. At age 19, he was released three years after having been accused of a crime for which he was never tried. There was an old running joke we had in my neighborhood growing up that we used in situations like this. It was a spin on words. We used it often when friends were jailed whom we knew were innocent: **There is no justice in America, just us.**

**While there is a racial component to the American justice system that leans more heavily on minorities, there is also a matter of resources involved.**

I would like to compare and contrast the Kalief Browder saga with that of Ethan Couch. Young Mr. Browder and his family had no resources to post bail or hire legal representation. This would contribute to the physical and emotional damage visited upon him which cost him his life. Let's take a look at life from the other side of the spectrum.

Affluenza was coined by a psychologist in a juvenile court to defend a wealthy Ethan Couch who was responsible for the deaths of four people in.

The psychologist argued that the young man was affected by affluenza. The malady was described as a mental illness which manifests itself through irresponsibility caused by family wealth which inhibits one from understanding consequences of negative actions.

Couch, the defendant who was 16 at the time of the crash, had a blood-alcohol level content three times above the legal limit for adult drivers. Despite the evidence, he avoided incarceration for the intoxication manslaughter charges. Once again, a member of the Couch family avoided justice by receiving 10 years of probation for his crime. Frank Miles of Fox News writes; "Ethan Couch, the Texas defendant who used the *'affluenza'* defense to get off on charges that he killed four people while drunk driving in 2013, was in legal trouble again earlier this year. His entire family has a history of breaking the law. The Couches' legal woes date back to at least the late 1980s, records show. Long before Ethan Couch and his family became notorious for using the *'affluenza'* defense, they had multiple run-ins with the law, often flouting authority or relying on personal wealth to get out of trouble. The incidents, totaling at least 20, ranged from speeding tickets and financial disputes to reckless driving and assault, a review of police and court records shows."

The disparity in the treatment of Kalief Browder and Ethan Couch exemplifies the broken social contract within the court system. There must be a replacement for cash bail, which is not an equitable or viable system for all Americans. Many poor defendants plea bargain their cases down to a lesser offense to avoid the tribulations that Mr. Browder faced. In fact, some of those who plead out are innocent, but are saddled with a criminal record from the plea deal.

It is believed by many that a lack of resources is the driving force behind criminality. To a certain degree, there is truth in that line of thinking. Poverty is definitely a root cause for many crimes. There are modern day situations every day that play out the same as that of Les Misérables. The focal point of the story is of Jean Valjean, who is starving and steals a loaf of bread. After spending 19 years in prison for his crime, you now have a hardened streetwise criminal who does not believe in the unjust system which has so negatively impacted his life. If we rid the prisons of non-violent drug offenders, America would be a very different place. The Assistant Director/General Council of the Federal Bureau of Prisons, Ken Hyle surmises that, "Based on FY 2020 data, the average annual Cost of Incarceration Fee (COIF) for a Federal inmate in a Federal facility in FY 2020 was $39,158 ($120.59 per day). The average annual COIF for a Federal inmate in a Residential Reentry Center for FY 2020 was $35,663 ($97.44 per day)" (*The Federal Register,* 2021, para. 3).

Imagine the growth of our economy if we had these inmates as tax paying citizens rather than a strain on the economy.

Having constructed this book using a sociological perspective, I would be remiss to leave out the social conflict theory. Conflict theory is a socio-political theory first espoused by Karl Marx. His theory was an effort to illuminate political and economic events in relation to a never-ending struggle over dwindling resources. At the apex of this struggle is the antagonistic relationship between social classes. Marx clearly defined social strata describing the relationship between the owners of capital—who Marx calls the ***bourgeoisie***—and the working class, which he calls the ***proletariat.***

Conflict theory had a profound influence on 19th- and 20th-century thought and continues to influence political debates to this day. The earlier illustration of judicial treatment between two 16-year-olds, Kalief Browder and Ethan Crouch, is a transparent example of the differences in how the classes are treated.

So, what happens when two individuals from opposite sides of the social strata are convicted of the same crime? Two words: *sentence disparity*.

Sam Levin, (2016) writes: "Raul Ramirez, a 32-year-old immigrant from El Salvador who admitted to sexually assaulting his female roommate in a case that has similarities with the Stanford case, was sentenced to three years in state prison under a deal overseen by judge Aaron Persky, according to records obtained by the Guardian.

The three-year-prison sentence, part of a plea agreement signed in March, provided a sharp contrast to the outcome for Turner, a white 20-year-old former Stanford swimmer who Persky sentenced to probation and six months in county jail after he was convicted of sexually assaulting an unconscious woman." (Levin, 2016, para. 2-3).

According to most literature on criminology, Frank Tannenbaum's theory known as "The Dramatization of Evil" was the first verbalization of the causes of deviation. His approach to deviance in the 1960s became known as the "labeling theory". Labeling theory is critical to understand deviant and criminal actions. It is bolstered by the assumption that no act is inherently criminal. Definitions of criminal behavior are established by those in power through the formulation of laws and the interpretation of those laws by police, courts, and correctional institutions. This analysis is congruent with the social contract in which the individual gives up certain rights for protection by the government. The problem is that the laws and courts are not just and do not provide a valid social contract.

A look at the disparity in sentencing levied by judge Persky makes it easy to see that our current system is broken when the same law is interpreted differently due to the defendant's race and socio-economic status. The Journal of Criminal Justice Volume (2009) states:

The empirical sentencing literature has focused intensively on racial equity concerns, but this research added to the literature by analyzing political-contextual sources of punishment. This study developed a functional model of court decision-making and used ordinal logit to assess court punishment decisions in 387 counties across seven states. The findings supported established assumptions about individual level punishment determinants but showed that political environment indicators also predicted sentence severity. Interactions were present as well. In law-and-order environments, Black defendants received harsher sentences, but in jurisdictions with the largest Black populations, Black defendants faced reduced punishments. With individual and state level effects held constant, the findings from this research reinforced claims that punishment is intensely political.

As with any political institution, valid and fair elections are imperative to a healthy operating environment. Currently in this country, some judges are elected while others are appointed by political entities. Unfortunately, some of the appointed judges serve for life. In a democratic society, it is a failure to address the needs and desires of the people, yet not give them input on selecting judges who have such a crucial impact on how the law is interpreted and administered.

Cornell Law School defines an officer of the court as, "Any person who has an obligation to promote justice and uphold the law, including judges, clerks, court personnel, police officers, and attorneys (who must be truthful in court and obey court rules)." If a social contract with the courts is to be valid, then individuals who are described as officers of the court must be beyond reproach in word and deed. After all, it is their words and actions that can impact an individual's freedom. Unfortunately, many officers of the court fail to meet the bar of honesty and service to all. As an example, here is an incident from Harris County Georgia that was surprising to some, but not the minority community served by the officers involved.

Excerpted below is news story by Nicole Carr:

"HAMILTON. Ga. — New video has surfaced showing more of a racist rant between a Georgia police chief and officer that has gotten national attention. The nation heard two Hamilton, Ga. police officers throw around the N-word, fantasize about slavery and make lewd remarks about preferred sexual contact with Black women. The video also shows officer John Brooks say he's counting on armed white people to handle protesters.

Ahead of a Black Lives Matter protest in Hamilton, Allmond and Brooks said the fatal police shooting of Rayshard Brooks was justified. 'Then how come when you tase a f---ing n-----, It's like you done killed him 27 times?' Brooks said.

Brooks made lewd sexual comments about Atlanta Mayor Keisha Lance Bottoms and Stacey Abrams. The men also reasoned that slavery is something in which Black people should be grateful when Allmond said in the video, "For the most part, it seems to me like they furnished them a house to live in. They furnished them clothes to put on their back. They furnished them food to put on their table, and all they had to do was f---ing work" (Carr, 2021, para. 1-8).

When the top police officer of a law enforcement organization openly expresses himself with this type of attitude, it is difficult to believe that he would treat minorities with the respect and fairness that all citizens should receive. As leader of the department, it is easy to surmise what he teaches his officers in relation to serving the community. Men like those illustrated in the Carr article should never be officers of the court. Unfortunately, in many places around the country, they are.

How about a few initiatives to mitigate some of the glaring problems described in this chapter? When it comes to law enforcement agencies, earlier in the book we prescribed civilian review boards and effective evaluation systems as part of a holistic healing process to fix the broken social contract. Another fix would be prohibition of qualified immunity. If officers understand that they will be held accountable for malfeasance, they will consider their actions in a more responsible manner. Additionally, no more appointments of judges; all should be elected, ending lifetime tenure for judges at every level.

Forbes describes what happens when judges who are out of step with mainstream America are appointed to the highest court in the land when it reported that 65% of American adults disapproved of the Supreme Court's overturning of Roe v. Wade in a July 2022 poll by the Kaiser Family Foundation. 25% of American adults wanted their state bans on abortion. The poll also reported 32% of those polled who reside in states that still uphold pre-Roe v. Wade abortion bans or "trigger laws"

"65%. That's the share of U.S. adults who disapprove of the Supreme Court overturning Roe v. Wade, a Kaiser Family Foundation poll released in July found. Only 25% want their state to ban abortion—including only 32% in states where the procedure is banned—while 51% want state laws that guarantee access (Durkee, 2022, para. 2-3).

Supreme court justices are all appointed to terms for life. It is difficult to argue for the effectiveness of the court when only 25% of the population agrees with such an important court decision. Appointments are strictly political, with the aim of furthering a political party's agenda, not being responsive to the desires and needs of the people. The system is totally broken and supports no social contract with working class Americans.

With the overturning of Roe v. Wade, the conservative majority of the Supreme Court has asserted that women no longer will have the right to control their own bodies. This verdict is a slap in the face for all women in this country and will negatively impact generations, unless the people force themselves to be heard.

This shift in paradigm is a dangerous precedent with tentacles that will grip the whole country by making women second class citizens. More than half of the women in this country now live in states that will make abortions illegal. The outcome is that women will lose access to safe reproductive health care. As usual, lower-income women who do not have the resources to travel for abortion care will be the hardest hit by this ill-conceived and malicious action that some politicians have been pushing for 50 years.

Without access to safe abortions at a medical facility, some women will die because of the supreme court's decision to overturn Roe vs. Wade. While Roe has been the law of the land for nearly 50 years, three generations of women have come to assume legalized abortion as a right. To have this right taken away by a few conservative judges is blatantly unfair.

Another caveat that must be considered when pondering the high court's decision to overturn Roe vs. Wade is the responsibility of the court. Per our constitution, it is congress that makes the laws and the courts responsibility to interpret those laws. That being said, for the court to overturn a precedent of 50 years appears to be an overreach. The supreme court has attained too much power with no real controls to ensure they are serving the American citizens.

The last component to be addressed in this chapter is the U.S. Congress. While the congress does not interpret the law, it makes the law. The current system under which U.S. Representatives operate is not a viable social contract. Events of the last few years have proven that many elected officials are more concerned with attaining and maintaining power than serving the people.

In a real-world version of Mr. Smith Goes to Washington, more than half of the members in Congress are millionaires. While many of the elected officials initially start their terms with lofty ideals of helping the working-class individuals who voted them into congress, this tends to change over time. The longer lawmakers stay in congress, the more out of touch with their constituents they become. Findings from the lawmakers' 2020 financial disclosures establish that the median net worth of Congress members who filed disclosures was slightly over $1 million.

While much of the wealth in Congress is concentrated in the hands of the top 10 percent, the longer individuals serve, the more wealth they generate. The wealthiest lawmakers have three times more wealth than the bottom 90 percent. The group of wealthiest members includes career politicians who have increased their affluence over decades in Congress. Attained wealth and security often blurs the lines of what constituents need in favor of what the representatives have.

A primary cause of bankruptcy in America is from medical expenses. All other industrialized nations have universal healthcare. Their systems tend to be proactive rather than reactive, and the results are positive. The U.S. healthcare system ranks from 21 to 30, depending on which agency is measuring. How can the richest country in the world be so far behind other nations? One reason is that the system that serves lawmakers is much different than that of the everyday citizen.

Robert Moffit writes for the Heritage Foundation, "Millions of Americans may be anxious about the cost and long-term security of their job-related health benefits. And over 35 million Americans worry because they have no health insurance coverage at all. But not members of Congress, their staff, and other federal employees.

They enjoy special health care privileges that are denied to the rest of Americans.

Members of Congress and other federal jobholders can choose from among dozens of alternative health plans each year, irrespective of their families' health condition. And when federal workers move to different jobs within the federal sector, they are able to keep the coverage of their chosen plan without any interruption of benefits. They can even keep their chosen plan when they retire. Few other Americans enjoy such healthcare security.

Congressmen, like other federal workers, understandably like their system. So much so, that buried in many of the leading bills to restructure the United States' healthcare system, there are provisions that quietly would exempt members of Congress, their staffs, and their dependents from each bill's effect" (Moffit, 1992, para. 1-2).

Insurance companies enjoy windfall profits of which some is used to lobby lawmakers to ensure the status quo. We must create a system that truly represents the ideals "Of the People, By the People, For the People". There is a growing number of Americans who are starting to lobby for term limits, as a method of mitigating the problems with our law-making body.

A summary of Dan Greenberg's report posted on the Heritage Foundation's site states:

"It is difficult to overstate the extent to which term limits would change Congress. They are supported by large majorities of most American demographic groups; they are opposed primarily by incumbent politicians and the special interest groups which depend on them. Term limits would ameliorate many of America's most serious political problems by counterbalancing incumbent advantages, ensuring congressional turnover, securing independent congressional judgment, and reducing election-related incentives for wasteful government spending. Perhaps most important,

Congress would acquire a sense of its own fragility and temporariness, possibly even coming to learn that it would acquire more legitimacy as an institution by doing better work on fewer tasks" (Greenberg, 1994).

There are currently 17 states that have fully legalized marijuana. Recently, President Biden announced that he will vacate all sentences at the federal level for those incarcerated for simple marijuana possession. The United States of America has more people incarcerated than any other nation in the world. Many of those are in prison for simple marijuana possession. Imagine the change in the country's Gross Domestic Product if these citizens were freed from prison and reintroduced to the job force. Instead of tax dollars being used to pay for incarceration, those dollars could be used to repair an aging infrastructure.

History repeats itself if it is ignored. During the age of prohibition, gangs made millions of dollars selling illegal alcohol. Uber violent gangsters made the streets unsafe as they used machine guns, bombs and other weapons to fight for control of the alcohol trade. The drive by shooting was invented during this time, and many innocent civilians were killed in the gang's crossfire. Sounds familiar? By legalizing and regulating marijuana, it would take away a large part of the revenue that gangs need to sustain themselves, decrease violence, and provide tax dollars that could be used to improve lives.

Politico journalist Natalie Fertig writes:

"Senate Majority Leader Chuck Schumer's Cannabis Administration and Opportunity Act would decriminalize weed on the federal level and allow states to set their own marijuana laws without fear of punishment from Washington.

The legislation includes both Democratic and Republican priorities: It expunges federal cannabis-related records and creates funding for law enforcement departments to fight illegal cannabis cultivation. It also establishes grant programs for small business owners entering the industry who are from communities disproportionately hurt by past drug laws, requires the Department of Transportation to research and develop a nationwide standard for marijuana-impaired driving, and restricts the marketing of cannabis to minors" (Fertig, 2022, para. 2, 4).

If congress was responsive to the needs of the people, marijuana legislation would be one of the top items on the legislative slate. Unfortunately, there are too many lobbyists who want to see the prison industrial complex filled with as many people as possible.

Nicki Lisa Cole, Ph.D. writes for Thoughtco:

"Foucault's key intellectual contribution was his deft ability to illustrate that institutions--like science, medicine, and the penal system--through the use of discourse, create subject categories for people to inhabit, and turn people into objects of scrutiny and of knowledge. Thus, he argued, those who control institutions, and their discourses wield power in society, because they shape the trajectories and outcomes of people's lives. Foucault also demonstrated in his work that the creation of subject and object categories is premised on hierarchies of power among people, and in turn, hierarchies of knowledge, whereby the knowledge of the powerful is considered legitimate and right, and that of the less powerful is considered invalid and wrong. Importantly, though, he emphasized that power is not held by individuals, but that it courses through society, lives in institutions, and is accessible to those who control institutions and the creation of knowledge. He thus considered knowledge and power inseparable, and denoted them as one concept, 'knowledge/power'" (Cole, 2019, para. 8-9).

I agree with much of Foucault's work. But I must add that institutions like the courts do have the power to impact individuals' lives. It is money and resources that determine how much control institutions have over a citizen.

Chapter 4

# Misapplications

Some things stick in an individual's mind forever. Interactions and observations can change the mindset in ways only that person can understand. These are defined as "Significant Emotional Events" (SEE) The theory was espoused by the sociologist Dr. Morris Massey.

Early one Sunday morning, I was on patrol in my cruiser when I received a call. The dispatcher sent me to a call in a residential neighborhood adjacent to a mental facility. I was told that there was a naked woman walking through the neighborhood. Arriving on the scene, within five minutes of the call, to my dismay, there was a woman walking in the middle of the street with only her bra and underwear on. Quickly looking in my trunk, I retrieved a jacket as it was very cool that morning. Wanting to provide some semblance of modesty, I offered it to her. Her response shook me, her body tensed as she squared up and looked me in my eyes as the only words she spoke were "I will kill you." The voice in which she spoke, and her eyes made the hair on the back of my neck stand up.

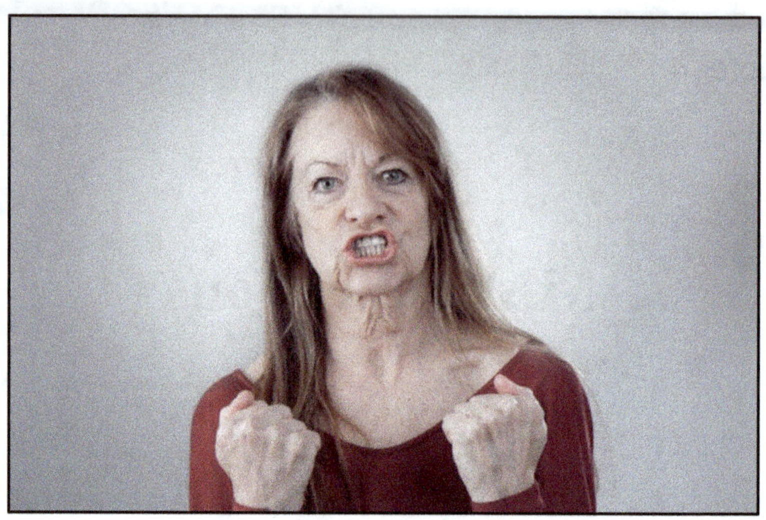

*She squared up and looked me in my eyes as the only words she spoke were:*

**"I will kill you."**

Assessing the situation, the call for backup was made as I gave ground to create space between us. The woman kept moving towards me and I felt a fence on my back. My observations told me that she was somewhere around 220 pounds, fairly fit, and not in a stable state of mind. While I did not feel she could beat me, I felt that if I engaged with her physically, I would have to hurt her to eliminate her as a threat. The minute she saw my back hit the fence she sprinted towards me. Throwing my jacket over her head and sidestepping, I was able to push her up against the fence, grab my pepper spray and once again create distance. She threw the coat to the ground and charged me again. Spraying her with the oleo-capsicum-resin produced the desired effect of incapacitating her. Opening my trunk, I retrieved a five-gallon water can to wash the resin off of her and waited for assistance. My section sergeant arrived, and when an attempt was made to help her, she became combative again. At this point, I took her back to the mental institution.

I have been fighting since elementary school. I learned how from an older cousin, Robert Johnson, whose skill with his hands was well known in our neighborhood. One of the things he taught me was to never be afraid. Fear clouds the mind and gives the upper hand to your opponent. I was in kindergarten when he shared this knowledge with me, and it helped me throughout my lifetime up until the day I met the naked woman. Individuals in her state can exhibit abnormal strength and a resistance to pain that gives them an advantage in a tussle. What has never left my mind since that interaction was her eyes. She had the look of a wild animal trying to escape. It was as if I was between her and freedom. No tears came from her eyes, even after having been pepper sprayed.

When the interaction was concluded and I was once again alone, many things ran through my mind. At one point I began crying. Emotions flowed through me that were conflicting and confusing. Feelings of sadness overwhelmed me as I was upset about having to pepper spray someone who was mentally unbalanced. Yet, I was happy that it was me she encountered. In my heart, I know that some officers would have beaten her with a baton or even shot her. Rarely do I write about my own experiences, but this situation held two-fold importance. 1. Each officer is different. Prior experience molds personality and determines the perspective from which the officer operates. 2. All officers are human and each carries with him or her the frailty of being such.

Police need either to be trained for or not used as first responders for a person known to be mentally ill. Services for the mentally ill are woefully inadequate and this needs to be addressed to cut down on the type of interactions as the one with the naked woman.

Having served in units such as the 2nd Infantry Division, 25th Infantry Division, and the 194th Armored Brigade, I developed a warrior mentality at a young age and lived it for over 22 years. The main job description for an Infantry soldier is to "close with and destroy the enemy". An Infantry soldier must have a warrior mindset, as it is crucial in order to stay alive and protect the team.

**Citizens are *not* the enemy**

I say there is no place in modern policing for a warrior mentality in the same mode that soldiers need. It is an officer's job to take care of and protect the citizenry. Cultivating a guardian mentality would be more beneficial to all. If there is a warrior mentality needed for policing, it was best described by the great Native American leader and warrior, Sitting Bull who stated:

"The warrior is not someone who fights, because no one has the right to take another life. The warrior, for us, is one who sacrifices himself for the good of others. His task is to take care of the elderly, the defenseless, those who cannot provide for themselves, and above all, the children, the future of humanity" (Historical Snapshots, 2023).

Seth Stoughton also clarifies the idea of the warrior mentality in the Harvard Law Review Forum:

"Within law enforcement, few things are more venerated than the concept of the Warrior. Officers are trained to cultivate a 'warrior mindset,' the virtues of which are extolled in books, articles, interviews, and seminars intended for a law enforcement audience" (Stoughton et al., 2015, para. 1).

An article in *Police Magazine* opens with a sentence that demonstrates with notable nonchalance just how ubiquitous the concept is: '[Officers] probably hear about needing to have a warrior mindset almost daily.'

Modern policing has so thoroughly assimilated the warrior mythos that, at some law enforcement agencies, it has become a point of professional pride to refer to the 'police warrior.' This is more than a relatively minor change in terminology. Though adopted with the best of intentions, the warrior concept has created substantial obstacles to improving police/community relations. In short, law enforcement has developed a "warrior" problem (Stoughton, 2015). In this commentary, I first describe how law enforcement training and tactics reflect the warrior concept, identifying aspects of modern policing that, if not addressed, will continue to prevent or undermine efforts to improve public perceptions of police legitimacy. I join a growing chorus of voices contending that it is the Guardian, not the Warrior, that offers the appropriate metaphor for modern officers. Stoughton (2015) continues:

Drawing on that principle, I offer two practical changes to police training that have the potential to advance the ultimate police mission — promoting public security — in a way that fosters, rather than thwarts, public trust: requiring non-enforcement contacts and emphasizing tactical restraint.

I agree with Mr. Stoughton wholeheartedly. Law enforcement must develop trust within the community in order to be successful. Creating an adversarial relationship is the last thing that officers need to do. The police should be looked upon with respect as guardians who improve the lives of all in the community with their service and sacrifice. Chapter One addresses the origins and evolution of police work. The poison of those negative credos cannot be overcome if citizens look at law enforcement as a cudgel, or police stick, meant to rule rather than serve them.

The grifters' specialty is that of cheating others out of money. Grifters go by many names. Chiselers, defrauders, gougers, scammers, swindlers, and flim-flam men. Selling a public building or conducting a Ponzi scheme are things a grifter might do. The difference between a grifter and a thief is that a grifter finesses victims out of their money through lies, while the thief takes it by force. In the end, the result is the same. I am not going to point fingers at anyone I mention in this book because mind reading is not in my skill set. But I am disappointed in some individuals who I feel are taking advantage of officers' fears and stressing a warrior mentality mindset as a panacea. Let's toss out the grifters who will do anything to make a dollar, no matter how harmful it may be to the community.

The warrior mindset contributes to negative interactions that often turn deadly for individuals who did not have to die. George Floyd, Michael Brown, and Tamir Rice were two unarmed Black men and a child, respectively, who were victims of unconscious bias and the warrior mindset. All are heartbreaking when viewed, but the killing of Tamir Rice illustrates the difference between Sitting Bull's description of a true warrior. and what law enforcement is being taught.

"At approximately 3:22 in the afternoon on November 22, 2014, City of Cleveland Division of Police (CPD) Communication Center received a 911 call advising that there was a 'guy in the park with a pistol, pointing it at people.' The caller who described the individual in question as a black male wearing a camo hat and a gray jacket with black sleeves, also stated that the individual was 'probably a juvenile' and the weapon was 'probably fake.'

Officers Garmback and Loehmann jumped the curb, traveled across the grass and came to a stop near a gazebo where an individual matching the description provided by dispatch was standing. Video surveillance at the park shows Officer Loehmann exiting the vehicle as the individual suspected to be armed reaches toward his right-side waist and lifts his jacket. Within one to two seconds of exiting the vehicle, Officer Loehmann fired his weapon twice from a distance of 4.5 to 7 feet, striking the individual in the abdomen. The individual, later determined to be twelve-year-old Tamir Rice, died the following day of the injuries he sustained. The weapon, which was in the possession of Tamir Rice at the time of the incident was an 'airsoft gun' with the orange markings of a toy removed" (Crawford, 2015, para. 2-4)

The officers involved in the shooting in this case showed tactical deficiencies and poor judgment, which contributed to the death of 12-year-old Tamir. The officer who shot the child called in to dispatch that Rice was a 20-year-old Black male. I have seen pictures of the child and there is no way he could be mistaken for a twenty-year-old, which is one hole in the officer's story. Secondly, if one fears that a suspect is armed, at no time would he or she pull the vehicle up to 4.5 feet of a suspect. It is impossible for the officer to have warned Rice three times in less than two seconds as he swore to in his statement. Incongruence between the officer's statements and the facts indicates that those officers did not see themselves as guardians. Conversely, the officer who fired upon the child forced a confrontation that was totally unnecessary. His warrior mindset caused him to take the life of a child who was no threat to anyone in the community.

To treat a human being as the police did Abner Louima is abhorrent and exemplifies the lack of a social contract between law enforcement and some members of society. Mr. Louima was a trained electrical engineer in his native country of Haiti. Immigrating to Brooklyn, he was a law-abiding citizen, husband, and father of one who worked hard as a security guard. One day, Abner was enjoying the nightlife and after visiting Club Rendezvous, an establishment in Flatbush, he and other patrons attempted to break up a fight between two women. D.L. Chandler stated:

"Police responded to the scene and tensions flared between the patrons and the officers, instigating a large scuffle. Officer Justin Volpe, the ringleader of the assailants in blue, and Charles Schwarz were among the first cops on the scene. Volpe incorrectly assumed Louima struck him with a sucker punch, leading all of the officers to beat the man with nightsticks, two-way radios, and their fists while taking him to the 70th Precinct holding cell.

Louima's evening would take a turn for the worse when the cops, drunken with anger, took him to a bathroom in the precinct and continued to beat him while Volpe kicked him and squeezed his privates. Volpe then took a plunger handle and sexually assaulted Louima, bragging to a fellow officer that he 'took a man down tonight,' according to the trial testimony" (Chandler, 2021, para. 4-5)

The brutality visited upon some citizens, the majority of whom are Black and Brown Americans, is congruent with the subhuman theory espoused by cultural anthropologist Nasir Uddin who has been working for years to build a new theory called "Subhuman Life" theory to understand the people living in acute, marginalized and atrocious conditions. 'Subhuman theory to juxtaposes the severely vulnerable condition of people in relation to an authoritarian nature of the state. It could also provide a new framework of understanding genocide, ethnocide, ethnic cleansing and homicide. Uddin argues that: "'subhuman' is a category of people who are born in human society, but have no space in the human community. 'Subhuman' does not receive treatments that a human deserves, and does not lead a life like a human being. 'Sub humans' are born in the world, but the world does not own them in any state-structure. 'Subhuman' are treated as *omanush* (non-human) since they do not exist in the legal framework of any state. 'Subhuman' is a particular category of people who live in the borderland of 'life' and 'death.' 'Sub humans' are not human beings in their due dignity, rights and voices, and are dealt with as if they are lesser than human beings."

Nearly a quarter of a century have passed, between the brutalization of Abner Louima and the murder of George Floyd, yet little has changed when it comes to law enforcement and the social contract. Mr. Floyd was removed from his vehicle by police officers after an accusation was made by a store owner. It is almost inconceivable that an officer would kneel on Mr. Floyd's neck for almost eight minutes while Mr. Floyd begged for his life, stating that he could not breathe. The crowd - kept away by other police officers - watched helplessly as Mr. Floyd pleaded for his dead mother to save him. There are many incidents similar to those suffered by Mr. Floyd and Mr. Louima due to our dysfunctional justice system; manned by some officers who feel they should rule, rather than serve citizens.

With the warrior mindset. some officers conflate their operating schema with that of a warfighter. Army, Navy, Air Force, and Marines train endlessly to become warfighters. The United States military is the best in the world, but not without sacrifice. Looking at mental illness and suicide rates among veterans proves that no amount of training can prepare the brain for violence and death of teammates and enemies. Servicemen and women put themselves in harm's way without hesitation, fighting to survive and keep teammates alive.

It was George S. Patton who pointed out that "the object of war is not to die for your country but to make the other bastard die for his."

Too bad it does not always turn out that way.

One of the most stressful and deadly acts for foot soldiers is fighting in urban areas. When clearing buildings of enemy forces, what's behind the next door could be the difference between life or death. It is in situations like these when the warfighter must overcome his fear, kick the door in, and execute the battle. Now, let's contrast those warfighters with law enforcement in a given situation such as the school shooting in Uvalde, Texas.

Reports indicate that there were in excess of 300 law enforcement officers at Robb Elementary School, the scene of the mass shooting incident. It would take those officers over an hour and 15 minutes to finally confront the shooter. There was much confusion as to who was in charge, and which tactics would be used to extract the shooter from the building. Herein lies one of the main differences between warfighters and law enforcement when it comes to a warrior mindset. Infantry soldiers, when operating in urban areas, realize that time is of the essence. The more time an adversary is given to prepare, to defend, and to position, the harder it will be to extract that individual. My heart sank as I observed the video of three officers running from a confrontation with the shooter after being fired upon. Those individuals were armed and had every opportunity to save the lives of those helpless children who were being held captive by the shooter. Tactics alone would have helped the officers at the scene if they were true war fighters. One effective method of contact would have been to dispatch a team outside of the building to break the windows of the classroom, thereby drawing the shooter's attention. While creating a distraction, they could have simultaneously used smoke, flash bangs, and 2-chlorobenzylidene malononitrile, (CS gas), to disorient and confuse the shooter from the outside of those windows. While the outside team is drawing the focus away from the children and the door, a breaching team could have been in place to take the door, make entry into the classroom, and eliminate the threat.

The fact that officers ran away from contact with the shooter is something I will never forget. The fact that it would take an hour and fifteen minutes, and over 300 reinforcements before the situation was quelled speaks volumes to the differences in the organization and skill level of warfighters and law-enforcement officers who feel they have a warrior's mentality.

It was exasperating, yet also eye-opening to observe the actions of some police officers when they faced a situation where the odds were not overwhelmingly in their favor. It's very easy for some officers to kneel on a man's neck for eight minutes knowing that he's dying when he has no means to defend himself. It's very easy for some officers to shoot an individual over 60 times when he's running away from them and has no means to defend himself. It's not so easy to enter the fray when faced with an armed adversary determined to cause harm. For those police officers, I say shame on you. We have to get away from this warrior mindset and move to what police should truly be, guardians of the community.

During the George Floyd protests, CNN's Hollie Silverman (2020) writes:

"Americans have been protesting the death of George Floyd at the hands of Minneapolis police for days on end in dozens of cities throughout the United States.

While tensions between police and demonstrators have heated up in many places, some officers have shown solidarity with the movement by hugging protesters, praying with them, mourning with them, and taking a knee to honor Floyd." (Silverman, 2020, para. 1-2)

These brave officers truly acted as guardians of the community. It is actions like theirs that are needed to build trust within the community for law-enforcement.

**Local law-enforcement officers have far too many responsibilities, which prohibit them from training in the manner that warfighters use to hone their skills.**

Just as a wrench. not a hammer, is used to remove or secure a bolt, an organization that trains for specific events will more often than not be the most effective. If we are not going to engage in gun control as a society, we must look into alternate means of protecting our communities from gun violence. I would recommend training and employing units specifically for mass shooter and domestic terrorist situations. We must stop using police officers as Swiss Army knives and allow them to focus on safeguarding the population and providing a safe environment for all, regardless of socioeconomic status or race.

Chapter 5

# Jail & Prison

I had the privilege to speak with education and activist Mr. Ernest Ward in preparation for a podcast. Mr. Ward has 30-plus years of experience and is a former leader of the NAACP in his county. Mr. Ward is one of the most intelligent individuals I have met and a tireless advocate for the underprivileged and under-represented in his community. Below is the transcript of our conversation:

**Mr. Ward:** What can be done to remove the barriers to Affordable Housing? What can be done to remove the barriers to a High Quality Fully Funded Education? What can be done to remove the barriers that allow full access to the Voting Ballot? What can be done to remove the barriers which deny access to a fair Judicial System? What can be done to remove the barriers that deny access to jobs with living wages?

**Me:** Excellent. I will structure the session to speak to all concerns.

**Mr. Ward:** These are the five most critical issues in the black community. These five areas have the ability to keep citizens from being homeowners and successful, productive citizens in the community.

**Me:** I agree wholeheartedly. I am currently writing a book about the justice system and the broken social contract. It befuddles me that a country with this many riches is okay with cultivating a permanent underclass through policies and laws.

**Mr. Ward:** The underclass is maintained by the elementary schools. The elementary schools lock students into a system of class based on poverty.

**Me**: That is an interesting theory. I never thought about it from that perspective.

**Mr. Ward:** I guarantee with you that it is more than a theory. It is a fact. The data shows that it is true. We send the poorest students in the community to the same schools. The communities these students live in have been neglected by the governmental municipalities when it comes to putting financial resources into these communities. The census data will show you that these are the poorest families who are in greatest need of resources, but they get the least. These are the same students that if you tracked them, you would see that they end up in jail more than any other community group. There is a system in place that is still working the systemic structure which was put in place by the philosophy of white supremacy.

Mr. Ward is speaking to parts of the insidious school to prison pipeline in a manner that most people have not been appraised of. He also brings into account how generational poverty contributes to incarceration. Make no mistake, the paradigm that he addresses is not accidental by any means, it is structural, systemic, and performing in the exact manner it was designed for.

Let us take a quick look at the consequences of the issues brought forth by Mr. Ward. We will compare the differences between jails and prisons prior to describing their impact on society.

Jails are normally local facilities under the jurisdiction of a county, local district, or city. They are short-term holding accommodations designed to house suspects who have been newly arrested, and those awaiting trial or sentencing. Normally, individuals sentenced to serve less than a year will be held in the local jail for the duration of their incarceration.

**Jails are normally local facilities under the jurisdiction of a county, local district, or city. Prisons, on the other hand, are organized and operated under the jurisdiction of the state or federal government.**

Prisons, on the other hand, are organized and operated under the jurisdiction of the state or federal government. These facilities are designed to house prisoners convicted of offenses that mandate sentences longer than one year. People who have been found guilty of breaking a state law are usually sent to a state prison. Those who have violated federal laws are normally sent to a federal prison located somewhere in the U.S. Some states have jails and prisons that are privately operated by a corporation. The state may contract with private organizations to house prisoners that may not exert the same level of control over how the facilities are operated as state-run prisons do.

Because they are designed for shorter stays, jails tend to have far fewer services than prisons. Inmates staying in jails are subject to insufficient medical care, poor dietary provisions, along with limited exercise and educational facilities which can severely impact inmate health both mentally and physically.

Inmates with previous legal issues and detainees awaiting trial who believe their cases may result in conviction are many times coerced to accept a plea in order to transition from jail to prison. This desire to leave the draconian conditions of jail and its many negative consequences has resulted in detainees, both innocent and guilty, accepting a plea that is not in their best interest.

One of the most unfair aspects of jail is the detention of innocent people. While it may be necessary in certain circumstances to detain individuals who are flight risks or pose a danger to the community before their conviction, our system, which maintains a presumption of innocence, should mean that they cannot be punished until their guilt has been proven. For those who cannot afford bail or legal representation, the harsh conditions of living in jail serve as de facto punishment.

One component of incarceration that is shared by both jails and prisons is violence. I have examined the ramifications at both the macro and micro levels.

Columbus is the second-most populated city in the state of Georgia, with the most populated city being Atlanta. Columbus has a population of 206,922 and an overcrowded jail with 1,120 inmates. When violence breaks out, more often than not gangs are involved, according to a news report by WRBL Senior Reporter Chuck Williams In it, then-Muscogee County Sheriff Donna Tompkins is cited as saying The Muscogee County Jail has had numerous attacks between inmates, and the majority of those are gang-related (Williams, 2018).

The rash of incidents reported above illustrates over-policing and unsafe jail conditions for the general public and traumatic and life-altering for victims like Mr. Earl Johnson who survived one of the assaults at the jail.

Mr. Johnson's ordeal began as a passenger in a vehicle that was pulled over for having tinted windows that were too dark. What normally happens in this situation results in the driver being given a ticket or a warning. For some reason, during this stop, people were removed from the vehicle, which was then searched.

A WTVM Channel 9 interview of Mr. Johnson's wife, Porchia, by Samantha Serbin (2019), indicated that a firearm was located under the driver's seat where a female was sitting. Mr. Johnson was arrested for violating probation and transported to the Muscogee County Jail despite no evidence of a weapon, drugs or any illegal item on his person, his wife said (Serbin, 2019).

After appearing in recorder's court and returning back to jail, Mr. Johnson was attacked by several gang members. He was stabbed in one eye and had his other eye gouged. The attack left him blind and with few answers from authorities such as Major Joe McCrea, an administrative bureau commander with the sheriff's office who "couldn't discuss any of the details" (Serbin, 2019, para. 7.

Mr. Johnson's release from the hospital with an unknown prognosis was met with frustration at the system that caused it:

"We're paying money to get the roads paved, that's not a necessity. I mean something like that is more important than driving on a road, building another building, security at a prison. They need security. I did not know he was going to go in walking, talking, singing, being hisself, to coming out relying on some help" (Serbin, 2019, para. 8).

Most citizens would agree with Mrs. Johnson that protecting those under supervision of any law enforcement agency should be paramount. Due to overcrowding, mixed with a lack of training and an uncaring attitude of some guards, jails and prisons in America are very dangerous places to be.

Take this report by Jens Modvig of the World Health Organization (2014):

1. "Prisons are violent places compared to the community. United States government statistics demonstrate that rates of physical assault for male inmates are more than 18 times higher than the equivalent rates for

males in the general population. For female inmates, the rates are more than 27 times higher. Violence in prisons is and should be a prison management and prison health service priority issue for several reasons. First, violence begets violence, that is, exposure to violence during adolescence increases the risk of later violent and non-violent crime, drug use and intimate violence against or from a partner. Thus, the rehabilitation or corrective dimension of imprisonment is undermined if prisoners are placed in an environment that makes them more violent and more criminal than before" (p. 19).

Every day law-abiding citizens who are placed in situations as described by Modvig, are forced to change their moral code when placed in gang-infested violent environments. Some are forced to join gangs for the purpose of survival. Once in a gang, getting out may be a very difficult and dangerous thing. It is likely that these detainees may develop a criminal mindset that changes the trajectory of not only their lives, but their loved ones as well.

In the American judicial system, citizens are promised a speedy trial. One of the reasons for our overcrowded jails is that that promise is not being kept. Individuals wait for months and sometimes years before they have their day in court. Some of these people are innocent, yet they are deprived of their freedom which in itself is a punitive state of being. As described in the Muscogee County incident and the Kalief Browder story, physical violence can change one's life forever. Not only do working class individuals who cannot afford bail or legal representation face the pitfalls of jail, they are no longer able to support a family; so, spouses and children suffer. This all feeds back to the systemic, white supremist actions described by Mr. Ward.

I find it hypocritical that the United States can sanction other countries for human rights abuses, when despite making up only about 5% of the global population, the U.S. has more than 20% of the world's prison population.

*Many of those incarcerated are imprisoned for non-violent drug offenses.*

Many of those incarcerated are imprisoned for non-violent drug offenses. It is inconceivable that a person in the state of Georgia will be convicted of a crime for possessing the same amount of marijuana that may be legally purchased and enjoyed in 17 other states in the country.

In order for the system to work effectively, the prison population must be reduced. There are other methods of rehabilitating non-violent drug offenders, and those involved in minor crimes that are not a danger to the community. This is especially true for women.

A growing problem is the care of incarcerated women who are pregnant in most states, according to Roxanne Daniels's briefing for the Prison Policy Initiative (Daniels, 2019).

"The National Commission on Correctional Health Care (NCCHC) has published a set of standards for the treatment of pregnant women in prison such as appropriate medical examinations as a component of prenatal care, specialized treatment for pregnant women with substance use disorders, and limited use of restraints throughout the course of the pregnancy. (A handy summary of the NCCHC's standards is available from the Nursing for Women's Health Journal, and the NCCHC's full position statement provides additional context.)" (para. 7).

The Eighth Amendment to the Constitution mandates prenatal care for all U.S. prisons and jails, but no specific government criteria have been established to guarantee that women are actually receiving the [appropriate] care they require (Daniels, 2019). Often, though, states fail to make their Department of Corrections policies publicly available, or even write guidelines on the care of incarcerated pregnant women in the first place. Despite the work of advocacy groups like the Rebecca Project for Human Rights and the American Civil Liberties Union (ACLU), previous attempts to track available policies in each state show that significant information gaps remain.

Additional research in the matter of jail pregnancies was very disheartening. Research indicates that a scarcity of codified procedures pertaining to the treatment of pregnant women in state prisons is a nationwide problem. In circumstances where protocols did exist, many times they were not sufficient to support the needs presented by pregnancy.

When prenatal care is examined, the lack of transparency by most states is alarming. Statistics in many instances are impossible to obtain. Prenatal care has been proven to be a primary tool for ensuring the health of the baby and mother. To not provide adequate measures which guarantee the most positive outcome for mother and child is despicable. Socio-economic circumstances multiply maladies such as STD's, insufficient diet, and substance abuse. These problems make complications during pregnancy more prevalent for women prisoners when compared to the general population.

Although the shackling of pregnant women has been documented to be a harmful practice, it is still used widely in many institutions. Childbirth, with no assistance, by women in their cells, has happened on many occasions due to a lack of diligence by prison staff. Some women have even been put in restraints while giving birth.

One accepted paradigm is that a country can be judged on how it treats its most vulnerable citizens. If that is true, we are failing as a nation. It is shameful how we treat expectant mothers and their unborn children. Another vulnerable demographic of our population, that is a target of abuse when incarcerated, is the mentally ill.

The Treatment Advocacy Center, Office of Research and Public Affairs stated, "Serious mental illness has become so prevalent in the US corrections system that jails and prisons are now commonly called 'the new asylums.' In point of fact, the Los Angeles County Jail, Chicago's Cook County Jail, or the New York's Rikers Island Jail Complex each hold more mentally ill inmates than any remaining psychiatric hospital in the United States. Overall, approximately 20% of inmates in jails and 15% of inmates in state prisons are now estimated to have a serious mental illness. Based on the total inmate population, this means approximately 383,000 individuals with severe psychiatric disease were behind bars in the United States in 2014, nearly 10 times the number of patients in the nation's state hospitals.

## BACKGROUND

In 44 states, a jail or prison holds more mentally ill individuals than the largest remaining state psychiatric hospital; in every county in the United States with both a county jail and a county psychiatric facility, more seriously mentally ill individuals are incarcerated than hospitalized.

### Serious Mental Illness (SMI) IN JAILS

A 2009 study based on inmate interviews conducted in Maryland and New York jails reported that within the month previous to the survey, 16.7% of the inmates (14.5% of males and 31% of females) had symptoms of a serious mental illness (schizophrenia, schizoaffective disorder, bipolar disorder, major depression or brief psychotic disorder). However, 31% of the inmates who were asked to participate in the study refused, a subset that almost certainly included many individuals with paranoid schizophrenia. The interviews were conducted between 2002 and 2006. Given the continued growth of mental illness in the criminal justice system, since that time and with the high rate of refusers in the survey, it is reasonable to estimate that approximately 20% of jail inmates today have a serious mental illness" (Carroll, 2016, para. 3).

As described at the beginning of this chapter, I was attacked by a mentally ill woman while working as a law enforcement officer. If charged with assaulting a police officer, she would have spent a significant amount of time incarcerated. I am grateful that her encounter was with me, rather than someone with a lack of empathy. It would have benefited no one if I had arrested her and charged the woman with a felony. Not only does America have a problem with penal institutions housing a disproportionate percentage of mentally ill, but every year, our streets are exponentially filled with homeless individuals; many who suffer from mental illness.

It is a systemic issue that must be rectified when mentally ill Americans are often denied the treatment they need, and instead end up in prisons and jails. The incarceration of mentally ill citizens happens so frequently that correctional facilities have become the de facto source for mental health services. Prison services tend to be woefully inadequate when it comes to treating mentally ill prisoners. Since most of these people will eventually be released, it is a danger to the general population as untreated mental issues tend to become worse. Statistics indicate that in a 40-year time frame, the prison population more than tripled from pre 1970s levels. As the prison population exponentially grew, the number of institutionalized mental patients decreased by 90% as resources to fund mental institutions were not budgeted for.

Alisa Roth (2020) probes deep inside of mental issues and prisons inside her exemplary work, *Insane: America's Criminal Treatment of Mental Illness*, she puts forth that half of all U.S. prisoners incarcerated are afflicted with mental illness. Her work indicates that this phenomenon occurs mainly due to a lack of other treatment options, indicating that they are more likely to end up behind bars than in a bonafide mental institution.

As suggested earlier, untreated mental illness, coupled with the harsh conditions of prisons, can create ticking time bombs with unknown triggers. It is widely understood that inmates with mental issues are targeted and abused at a higher rate than other prisoners. The trauma that they suffer can result in broken minds that are beyond repair. To release these individuals back into society without extensive treatment is a disservice to that person and a serious danger to society. No rational person can expect to see a positive reentry into the community by those who have coping deficiencies. This is especially true after they have been forced to live for years in inhumane conditions. In order to address this problem, the country must consider housing inmates with special needs in facilities designed to treat them and keep them away from predatory inmates. This would require an investment in new age mental institutions designed to house and treat the mentally ill who have committed crimes.

According to Galletta et al., (2021), "Few would dispute the notion that achieving successful reentry into society after an extended stay in prison is an extremely difficult process fraught with countless obstacles. Among those hurdles are access to adequate health care, acquisition of gainful employment, identification of affordable housing, and successful reintegration into the family and community. As challenging as the reentry process is for inmates in general, it is even more difficult for those with mental illness. These inmates face all the aforementioned obstacles but often to an even greater degree. This phenomenon is reflected in statistics revealing that mentally ill releases are significantly more likely than their mentally healthy counterparts to recidivate (Galletta et al., 2021 as cited in Baillargeon et al., 2009). Additionally, severity of mental illness has been correlated with likelihood to recidivate (Galletta et al., 2021 as cited in Bales et al., 2017). One major contributor to this statistic revolves around housing concerns. Inmates with mental illness are more likely than those without mental illness to be homeless after release (Galletta et al., 2021 as cited in Herbert et al., 2015). Common causes for homelessness among these inmates include lack of adequate community-based treatment programs, difficulty obtaining employment leading to financial inability to support housing, psychotic symptoms interfering with the organizational abilities required to obtain stable housing, and substance abuse resulting in allocation of financial assets to drugs over housing (Galletta et al., 2021 as cited in Draine et al., 2002; Folsom et al., 2005)

Employment outcomes are also much poorer for mentally ill inmates both before and after incarceration (Galletta et al., 2021 as cited in Baillargeon et al., 2010). In a 2008 study of ex-prisoners in Ohio and Texas, 53% of men and 35% of women without mental illness were legally employed (which excludes "under-the-table" work as well as working for a family member or friend) within 8 to 10 months of release, but among mentally ill ex-prisoners in the same samples, only 28% of men and 18% of women were legally employed.

There are three primary barriers that individuals with mental illness face when seeking and maintaining employment, regardless of the additional factor of a criminal history. The first is the interference of the illness itself with achieving occupational and social functioning levels necessary for the job (Galletta et al., 2021 as cited in Baron & Salzer, 2002). For example, depressive symptoms can negatively impact energy and overall mood; various disorders, including psychotic disorders, may cause interpersonal skills deficits that affect work relationships and client interactions; and cognitive deficits can hinder an individual's ability to solve problems and complete required work tasks (Galletta et al., 2021 as cited in Baron & Salzer, 2002). The second barrier is inaccessibility and inadequacy of mental health rehabilitation programs with an occupational focus (Baron & Salzer, 2002). The third is employer discrimination (Galletta et al., 2021 as cited in Batastini et al., 2017). Although the Americans with Disability Act offers protection from many forms of discrimination, informal discrimination, including negative workplace attitudes toward those with mental illness, still persists and is often not actionable" (Introduction).

## Federal Prison Security Levels

Alan Ellis (2016) describes the classification of the federal prison system: "In the Bureau of Prisons, each federal prison institution falls into one of five different security levels" (para.3)

- Minimum
- Low
- Medium
- High
- Administrative

The Table below (Federal Bureau of Prisons, 2023) shows the most current statistical data of the federal prison population as of July 29, 2023.

| Security Level | # of Inmates | % of Inmates |
| --- | --- | --- |
| Minimum | 23, 285 | 14.7% |
| Low | 56,030 | 35.5% |
| Medium | 53.430 | 33.8% |
| High | 19,536 | 12.4% |
| Unclassified | 5,609 | 3.6% |

The term "Unclassified" describes prisoners who are still waiting to receive a security level.

As the levels of prisons and assignment criteria are explained, the Dickensian aspect once again comes into play. Many who have committed white collar crimes are housed in minimum security facilities. We are, in some instances, having to wrap our brains around seeing individuals who have stolen millions of dollars and destroyed the security and lifestyles of people around the country assigned to minimum security work camps. Individuals assigned to these penal institutions enjoy freedoms and privileges that mainstream inmates can only dream of. How can one reconcile those inmates living in comfort while we have non-violent drug offenders who have harmed no one serving time under much harsher conditions. Prison assignments, once again, illustrate how wealth and power, rather than legitimacy, decides one's punishment in a broken justice system.

One level of lockup identified as Administrative in the Bureau of Prison's (BOP) graph is the supermax prison. Currently, there is only one supermax in the federal system. The maximum-security facility is located in Florence, Colorado, and it uses the ADX acronym, which stands for Administrative-Maximum US Penitentiary (prisons) as its designation. While there is only one supermax at the federal level, 44 states operate supermax facilities. Some argue that conditions in supermax facilities are not designed to rehabilitate, they are simply inhumane holding prisons. When exploring methods used to control prisoners, that is a valid thought process. Supermax maximum security prisons in most instances maintain inmates for as much as 23 hours per day in segregation. Life inside a supermax prison is one of the most highly regulated and psychologically destructive environments imaginable for prisoners. The supermax has no instruments for socialization, no job education, and access to natural light for most prisoners is not provided. A supermax prison cell is 7 feet by 12 feet in size. The prison is built primarily of poured concrete to prevent inmates from making weapons out of accouterments found in most prisons. The design also makes the building almost impenetrable and inescapable. The prison boasts remote-controlled steel doors, and the entire facility is surrounded by 12 feet of razor wire fencing. Other security surrounding the prison includes laser beams, guard dogs, pressure pads, and gun towers in addition to hundreds of cameras and motion sensors. While all super max institutions are not built exactly like ADX, most supermax units tend to follow similar architectural and security procedures.

The disorientation and sensory deprivation experienced by subjects housed in ADX, and similar lockups, is designed to make it difficult for inmates to know where they are at any given time and to limit their ability to see the outside world. The supermax environment is the perfect concoction for developing psychosis.

Wise (2019) describes the factors listed below that determine the level of a federal prison.

1. The use of mobile patrols to secure that institution's perimeter 24 hours each day 365 days a year.
2. Gun towers located around the prison's perimeter. Armed guards monitor the movement and activities from inside those gun towers. These guards are authorized to use deadly force.
3. Perimeter barricades that isolate the facility from its neighboring municipalities.

4. Passive devices like metal detectors to discourage the possession of weapons and other contraband. Active deterrents such as sound-guns that can intercept prisoner conversations.
5. Internal security that includes cameras locks on doors to control access, and bars on windows.
6. Choices of accommodations, such as whether the institution confines people in locked rooms, open dormitories.
7. The ratio of staff members to inmates.

As federal prison security levels increase, so do restrictions, at the same moment liberties decrease. The BOP also operates select, Special Management Units (SMUs), which are located within United States Penitentiaries. If an individual is sent to the ADX or an SMU, it's because authorities have deemed that individual as being predacious, or incapable of functioning in a more open prison environment.

The requirements for assignment to a minimum security institution the inmate must be within 10 years of the release date.

- Federal inmate must not have a documented history of violence or sex offenses.
- Federal inmate must not have any history of escape attempts.

Administrative-level facilities hold prisoners from any and all security levels. This means that convicted murderers will be serving time alongside tax evaders.

FEDERAL INMATE CRITERIA FOR BEING HELD AT THE ADMINISTRATIVE LEVEL:

1. Administrative facilities confine federal inmates who have active judicial proceedings. They are like large jails where people await transfer to a more permanent facility.
2. Administrative facilities confine federal inmates who need medical attention or special programming, such as Federal Medical Centers.

Many FMCs have affiliations with local hospitals in the neighboring communities.

3.  Administrative facilities confine federal inmates who are in transit from one institution to another. The primary transit center is the Federal Transit Center at the Oklahoma City airport.
4.  Administrative facilities confine federal inmates who authorities have classified as being especially dangerous or prone to escape, such as the administrative maximum unit in Florence or the Special Management Units, like the one at USP Lewisburg" (Wise, 2019)

United States Penitentiaries (USPs) are the most dangerous of all federal prisons. Federal prisoners who serve inside of a USP in many instances tend to be some of the most violent of all inmates incarcerated. Inside USP's, organized crime runs rampant. Gangs, not guards, dictate much of what goes on in the cell blocks. Unfortunately, individuals with mental issues as discussed earlier are targets of abuse, and are victimized and exploited at every turn.

As a consequence of sentencing laws that punish people extensively for high-dollar crimes, a relatively small percentage of people on the compound serve time for white-collar crimes. All federal prisoners in the penitentiary share common areas together. Federal prisoners live by a different code than exists in the world outside. The daily environment is filled with high levels of violence, manipulation, extortion, and alterations. Federal inmates serving time inside of USPs are militant and stubbornly resistant to authority. Volatility is a constant in a USP. Strict rules and schedules restrict all movement in a USP. If an individual is not assigned to a work detail, the individual may request access to the recreation yard, the education area, participate in table games in the housing unit, or watch television in a designated area. The environment is borderline tribal, with varying factions of federal inmates influencing activities inside. Federal inmates serving in USP witness routine violence. This will include the use of federal inmate created weapons, such as knives, blunt instruments, pipes and/or clubs. There is a high concentration of predatory, unstable individuals living in a USP; it is the worst possible place to serve time.

Medium-security prisons are known as Federal Correctional Institutions (FCIs). They confine prisoners from all backgrounds, and with all types of sentence lengths. Most of the people who serve time inside of a medium-security FCI will have extensive criminal histories, and many will serve sentences in excess of 30 years. Yet, all FCIs will include a population of offenders who serve sentences for sophisticated criminal activity that does not include street crimes. A medium-security FCI will be less volatile than a USP, confining between 800 and 2,000 people. For the most part, average sentence lengths will span between 10 and 30 years, although some people in medium-security FCIs will be serving life sentences. The institutions will have lower levels of violence, gang activities, and volatility, though those levels will still be too high for comfort. As in the penitentiary, the atmosphere squashes hope for many. Prisoners in a medium-security FCI will see and hear about violence routinely, though not on a daily basis as in the USP. Some of the violence will include the use of weapons that prisoners manufacture, like knives and blunt instruments like pipes or clubs. FCIs prove to be the second-worst possible place to serve time.

Low-security prisons are also known as Federal Correctional Institutions (FCIs). They confine federal prisoners from all backgrounds. Federal inmates in low-security FCIs do not have extensive, documented criminal history. If they have a history of violent behavior, several years have passed since the last documented act of violence. Prison administrators are known to (often) make classification errors, leading to the confinement of violent individuals in low-security institutions–institutions which confine well-educated, white-collar offenders.

A low-security FCI will be less volatile than either a medium-security FCI or high-security USP. Population levels will hold between 1,000 and 2,500 federal inmates. All prisoners in a low-security FCI will be within 20 years of their scheduled release date. There will be few organized disturbances, and gang activity will not likely intrude on the lives of non-gang members. Most of the federal inmates serving time inside a low-security FCI are focused on their release date and staying out of further trouble. If a federal inmate has been convicted of a sex offense, or if the individual has a history of cooperating with authorities, the individual will face challenges from staff and inmates alike.

## Living Quarters

Federal prisoners in low-security FCIs live in open dormitories. Bathrooms are in a common area, under the "open" plan. Federal inmates live in close proximity to each other and there are minimal levels of privacy. Federal prisoners in a low-security FCI face less instances of volatility than inmates in a higher security prison. It is highly unusual for federal prisoners in a low-security FCI to gather, riot or form an orchestrated disturbance. There are exceptions, but typically, violence in low security is sporadic and hardly orchestrated.

Federal Prison Camps (FPCs) are minimum-security camps that hold federal inmates who are within 10 years of their release date, do not have documented histories of violence, and do not have any record of escape attempts. FPCs may hold federal prisoners who started at a higher-security prison. Most white-collar offenders serve their time inside of minimum-security camps. That being said, the population inside minimum-security camps has a higher educational level. Still, every offender should do everything possible to position himself to serve his sentence in the best possible prison. The focus in the camp will be on returning home, as someone is released almost every day. Many of the federal inmates surrendered to camp voluntarily, which suggests that authorities perceive them as people who can be trusted. However, the low level of security causes administrators to experience a significant issue with the introduction of contraband. The high levels of contraband can be extremely tempting for federal inmates in minimum-security camps.

The Machiavellian, or scheming nature of America's jails and prisons indicate that the justice system has no intention of rehabilitating individuals who have been incarcerated. Prisons are one of the means of maintaining a permanent underclass to be exploited by the rich and powerful, whether those souls are in or out of the penal system. While many of us look at the criminal justice system and declare it broken, truly, it is not. For the rich and powerful, the system works exactly how it was designed to function. Money and power are used to suborn every layer of the legal system, from police on the street, to judges at all levels of the system, to politicians who make the laws. It creates situations like the affluenza case, allowing a rich youngster to walk away from multiple cases of vehicular manslaughter, free as the wind. During the crack epidemic, someone convicted in federal court of possessing crack cocaine would receive the same sentence as someone who possessed 100 times more powder cocaine. You might wonder what the difference is between crack and coke to justify this 100-to-1 ratio? Crack was consumed mainly by black and brown people who could not afford powder cocaine, the drug of choice for more affluent people. Between the addiction issues and harsh prison sentences handed down for crack, two whole generations of Black Americans were negatively affected directly. The communities from whence they came are dealing with the impact of their loss to this very day.

Many of those who observe the opioid epidemic today cry foul. Their observation is in the fact that demographics impacted by the two drugs are very different, and so are the approaches to eradicating both problems. The majority of those who abuse opioids are white. They are found across the country. Rather than fill the jails with these individuals, it is now said that addiction is an illness. Rather than mass incarceration of these offenders, many diversionary programs have been established for treatment, rather than prison, which was the solution for the crack epidemic.

# Chapter 6

# Punishment vs. Rehabilitation

Over the course of 65 years on this earth, to my dismay, some of my friends and family members have had the misfortune of being incarcerated. In some cases, those individuals were guilty of a crime or crimes; in other cases, they were not. Most distressing was the fact that the majority of their sentences were harsher than they should have been. I will share two cases to illustrate my point. I have an older uncle who was born and raised in Florida. Growing up in rural parts of the state, he, as did all of my uncles, had the knowledge and ability to live off the land. In the 1950's and 60's, jobs and money were extremely difficult to obtain for a Black man in that part of the country. He fell to the temptation of killing an alligator, with the intention of selling its meat and hide. He was arrested for the crime and spent seven years incarcerated in a work camp. While he was wrong and should have been punished, seven years from a man's life, seven years for killing an alligator is beyond the pale.

Someone I have known since birth, was always a happy, hardworking young man with no criminal record. One day, he became embroiled in an argument with two individuals. The man and his male companion jumped the young man and one of them attacked him with a knife. One attacker was killed, and the young man and the second assailant were both hospitalized with severe knife wounds. Lack of adequate legal representation for the young man, resulted in a 17 year prison bid in a maximum-security prison for an offense that he was not guilty of.

One element consistent with folks I know who have been incarcerated for long periods of time is a change of attitude and approach to life. It's as if some form of PTSD interferes with reestablishing relationships. Could you imagine what a significant emotional event it would be if for the next several years, you were housed with criminals and abusive guards while being innocent of the crime you were convicted of?

It's not just egregious in the sentencing and lack of justice but being subjected to the pitfalls of life in an American prison that negatively impacts most assigned to those institutions.

Most prisons in the country have some type of education system that offers high school and college programs for inmates. The problem lies in the fact that most employers balk at hiring convicted felons after they have served their time, no matter what degrees or certifications the individual may hold.

Parker Murphy (2020) writes: "Rehabilitation is a growing option that people believe will be a better alternative to punishing criminals and incarcerating them. 'Rehabilitation gives someone the chance to learn about his/her problems and offers one to learn how to change their behavior in order to not commit a crime'" (GadekRadek n.d., pg.1 as cited in Murphy, 2020).

Unlike incarcerating someone for their max jail time then throwing them back into society, rehabilitation is a way to ease the offender back into society. This is one of the biggest reasons people want to push this option, as to decrease recidivism and crime rates. There is evidence to show that rehabilitation methods have worked in the past. Such as in the late 1900s, rehabilitation was a prominent factor in the U.S prison system. As years went on, punishment became more prominent and crime rates grew.

"Rehabilitation is also wanted for the fact that prison systems do not give a person the help they need to get better. For example, if a person needs drug, alcohol, or violence rehabilitation they would get it through rehabilitative programs. "Today, somewhere between 15 and 20% of people in prison are mentally ill" (American Psychology Association n.d., pg. 1 as cited in Benson, 2003).

On the other hand, punishment and incarceration is the top option for people who commit crimes. "Punishment puts offenders in the confines of a cell in order to think about the crime he/she has committed (GadekRadek n.d., pg.1). People need to know there are consequences to their actions. If someone knows they will only have to go through a rehabilitative program and avoid physical time, they will not learn their lesson. Within the prison system, there are programs that the prisons can do such as having drug or counseling on how to be a better parent. One of the main reasons for punishment is so victim's families get closure. If a family member is taken from them, then they expect that the person who did it at least lose their freedoms. Another good aspect of incarceration is the fact that the prisoners can get their GED and education so when they are released, they can get jobs. Some educational opportunities are high school diplomas and vocational" (Murphy, 2020, para. 3)

Mr. Murphy wrote a very interesting piece about punishment versus rehabilitation. Much of what he states is factual. That being said, the dichotomy is not congruent with current ideas about prison reform. Rehabilitation does not mean that individuals should not be incarcerated for their crimes. Rehabilitation should be a part of the prison curriculum. Programs are needed in prison that educate those who are locked up, on being productive citizens who contribute to communities in a positive manner. Denying a person of their freedom should be enough of a punishment. To treat them as animals and, then, expect a positive reentry into mainstream society is a panacea that will never work. Penal institutions need to be reformed to provide a holistic approach that provides hard and soft skills needed to be a successful law-abiding citizen.

In jails and prisons that are controlled by gangs and some guards who are on the wrong side of the bars, it is a might-is-right and a dog-eat-dog world. No one should be expected to internalize these rules, live by them and upon release, adopt a totally divergent mindset and social register. In order for our prisons to be successful in extinguishing undesired behaviors, we must be more realistic in our expectations. That does not mean releasing super predators into the streets as our penal institutions currently do. By building true self-respect in prisoners, they can be taught a better way than walking the path that ends in self-destruction. There is currently one prison in the country that has figured out and implemented a better way.

"A Model Prison," reported by Robert F. Worth (1995) for *The Atlantic,* states, "Approaching McKean, the federal correctional institution in Bradford, Pennsylvania, one is not likely to think of a prison. The buildings, low and modern, display a pseudo-Navajo motif in soft gray and salmon colors. In the air-conditioned entryway there are carpets over an immaculate tile floor, the glimmer of polished glass, the green tint of tropical plants. Tasteful couches sit in the corners. Well-dressed employees walk up and down the stairs, speaking in hushed, respectful tones. Beyond, on the prison grounds, are a broad expanse of well-tended lawn and distant athletic fields. Inmates walk alone or in pairs along the concrete pathways, offering greetings as they pass. Across the compound, inmates sit quietly in classrooms, learning everything from basic reading skills to masonry, carpentry, horticulture, barbering, cooking, and catering. Next door is a multi-denominational chapel. The cell blocks are cramped but clean and orderly, with a weekly inspection score posted on the wall. 'With visitors, it's like a joke, to see how long before they compare this place to a college campus,' one prison staff member says. This prison and others like it are the targets of a fierce campaign that is changing the shape of the U.S. criminal-justice system. For several years journalists and politicians all over the country have spoken and written angrily about such prisons as 'resorts' or 'country clubs.' They have railed against a philosophy of rehabilitation that 'coddles' inmates with too many amenities. Punishment is in vogue, along with hard labor and 'no frills' prisons, stripped of weight rooms, TVs, and computers. Republicans in Congress have added a no-frills-prison section to the Contract with America's 'Take Back Our Streets Act,' and they have passed it as an amendment to the 1994 crime bill. Massachusetts Governor William F. Weld has argued that prisons should be 'a tour through the circles of hell,' where inmates should learn only 'the joys of busting rocks.' Alabama has already reinstituted the chain gang, forcing inmates to do hard labor in leg irons for up to ten hours a day. State administrators and sheriffs, sniffing the political wind, have begun to crack down, cutting educational and treatment programs, making prison life as harsh as possible."

Yet McKean, by several measures, may well be the most successful medium-security prison in the country. Badly overcrowded, housing a growing number of violent criminals, it costs taxpayers approximately $15,370 a year for each inmate. That is below the average for prisons of its type, and far below the overall federal average of $21,350. It is about two thirds of what many state prisons cost. And the incident record since McKean opened, in 1989, reads like a blank slate: No escapes. No homicides. No sexual assaults. No suicides. In six years there have been three serious assaults on staff members and six recorded assaults on inmates. State prisons of comparable size often see that many assaults in a single week. The American Correctional Society has given McKean one of its highest possible ratings. No recidivism studies have been conducted on its former inmates, but senior staff members claim that McKean parolees return to prison far less often than those from other institutions, and a local parole officer agrees. According to the Princeton University criminologist John DiIulio, 'McKean is probably the best-managed prison in the country. And that has everything to do with a warden named Dennis Luther.'"

Worth goes on to describe the physical appearance and demeanor of the warden, Mr. Dennis Luther. What stands out is the picture of a man that understands he does not have to talk loudly and carry a big stick in order to garner respect. He also understands that in order to gain respect, one must also show respect. He teaches those tenets to his staff, and they live by them.

According to the Worth, Mr. Luther has developed a systemic approach to constructing what he calls "prison culture." The warden spent years studying business models and developing a methodology which could be applied to prisons, making them more efficient and empathetic. By developing a culture that mitigates violence and eliminates gang control, Mr. Luther set his prison on the correct path of what rehabilitation is truly about.

One of the main items illustrated in the article pertains to the many positive reinforcement plaques that hang throughout the prison, buttressing the ideals and mores needed to become successful in the outside world. The prison is kept in an immaculate state, one that encourages the inmates to respect their surroundings. Both classical and operant conditioning are applied, with an emphasis of non-punitive measures whenever possible.

As a drill sergeant in the U.S. Army, we used very similar conditioning methods which have resulted in our armed forces being the best in the world. There is one critical difference between the military model and that developed by Mr. Turner. When inmates arrive in a prison, they are already at a low point in life. This allows for positive building of the psyche, almost immediately. In the military model, a drill sergeant begins soldier training by stripping them all down to their bare essence. Scenarios and structure then force them to learn to trust each other and work together. Progressively, harder tasks are introduced, which when overcome, builds confidence. Increasingly, the drill sergeants then cede more responsibility, and control to the trainees which builds the spirit, teamwork, and desire to reach their maximum potential. Numerous parents have come to me after graduation expressing thanks and stating that they never imagined their child becoming the man that they have been reunited with.

Warden Luther has prepared a template. This is the type of rehabilitation that is needed in our prisons today. Life skills, education and responsibility all must be packaged into the type of systemic holistic approach that will prepare inmates for reentry into mainstream society. Our current system results in one of the highest recidivism rates in the world. Reducing the recidivism rate would go a long way towards eliminating overcrowding in jails and prisons, thereby saving millions of dollars that could be used elsewhere in our society. Recidivism is defined as the predisposition of a convicted criminal to reoffend by committing a crime after serving their sentence for a previous conviction. As stated earlier this country has one of the highest recidivism rates in the world. The National Institute of Justice has concluded that approximately 44% of criminals released from prison have returned before their first year out of prison. In 2005, about 68% of 405,000 released prisoners were arrested for a new crime within three years, and 77% were arrested within five years. It is a totally unsustainable system when over seven out of ten inmates find their way back into the system.

In an effort to correct this broken system, it benefits us to study and emulate some of the countries that do well with correcting criminal behavior and mitigating recidivism.

Most citizens who have not been incarcerated have their own visions of what a prison should look like. These images have been formed mainly through media sources, especially television and movies. Many see prison as a violent and dangerous institution controlled by gangs. It is a place where lawbreakers go to receive punishment for crimes, not rehabilitation. What's sad is that in America, the descriptors above used to explain prison life are pretty accurate.

Some say that the definition of insanity is repeatedly doing the same thing and expecting a different outcome. America's prison system has been, and is, insane.

The Scandinavian countries including Norway have a recidivism rate of about 25% over a five-year period after release. One major reason is that the typical prison in Norway is totally different from those in the U.S. Those differences are why they have much better results in turning those who have committed crimes into productive contributors to society.

Rudy Gerhold from the Kent Partnership writes,

"Halden is a maximum-security prison within 75-acre land. It is also the second biggest of its kind in Norway and receives people from worldwide. However, it is also an interior design awardee and, most of all, one of the most liberal prisons.

In Halden, inmates live almost similar to the general population. They engage in a variety of activities, from sports to music. Their windows don't have bars, and they have easy access to sharp objects. The only difference is they're stuck there for some time.

Halden isn't the only prison to operate in this manner. So do the rest in Norway. While some have criticized this system, most call it the most successful—one worth emulating by American prisons" (para. 1-4).

The holistic approach to incarceration in Norway is consistent with the requirements of Maslow's Hierarchy of Needs (1943). The paradigm identified and espoused by Abraham Maslow uses a pyramid of stages that must be obtained prior to an individual becoming more invested in society and reaching a state of self-actualization. This level of being is the realization of an individuals' maximum potential and self-awareness. The drive for reaching the top level of the pyramid is an innate construct that is stifled by American prison structure, yet granted by the Norwegian model. Please examine the pyramid closely prior to continuing.

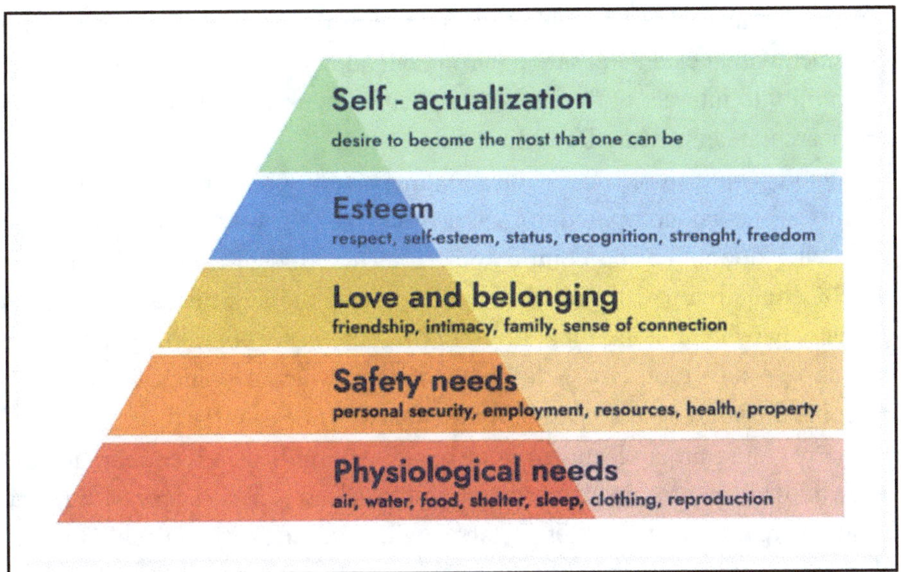


The end game of prisons in this country is punishment of the inmates. The focus of punishment without rehabilitation is short sighted due to the fact that it leaves individuals unable to contribute to society upon release. That inability to reintegrate into mainstream society results in overcrowding of prisons, partly caused by a high recidivism rate. It impacts the country's fiscal bottom line, as the taxpayers end up paying hard earned money to house inmates who could be tax paying citizens if they were rehabilitated and integrated successfully into mainstream society. Norway's system of restorative justice is designed to provide those individuals incarcerated with an opportunity to rehabilitate and become a contributing member of society. The hierarchy of needs is dependent on the items of one level being met before the next level may be realized. Due to overcrowding and antiquated design, the majority of prisons in this country do not provide an environment that satisfies level one, leaving all other levels unattainable.

While incarcerated Norwegians engage in many activities which aid them in leaving prison and living a life free of crime, those who need it are taught life skills, and some go to school. Most importantly, they are allowed frequent contact with their families and visitation with incarcerated loved ones twice a week; even spending time with them alone. Individuals are provided with a clean and safe environment, along with an adequate diet and the ability to interact with others in a positive manner. All of this results in an incarcerated individual's ability to move to the top of Maslow's pyramid.

One would think that if the treatment and conditions of Norwegian facilities is so lax compared to U.S. prisons, that Norway's jails would have revolving doors. To the contrary, the total recidivism rate in America is 76.6% compared to 20% in Norway. Let's stop making the same mistakes repeatedly while looking for a different outcome. If we continue with this eye for an eye and tooth for a tooth mentality, when it comes to issues in prisons, the country will be too blind to and toothless to fix them.

Providing an environment and positive stimuli which encourages the growth of spirituality is vital in creating the structure for a successful return to mainstream society. In this instance, when we speak of spirituality rather than religion, it is the insight which involves the recognition of a feeling or sense or belief that there are forces greater than self. It is the recognition of a symbiotic relationship whereby a larger community is dependent upon each of us realizing the connectedness that binds us. Spirituality also breeds self-love. This encourages the respect and empathy needed to reach self-actualization.

# Chapter 7

# Poverty

Poverty is the fuel that drives the American justice system. It impacts those who suffer from its effects from an early age. The school-to-prison pipeline refers to the tendency of schools to push students out of the education system and into the criminal justice system. This action is generated by harsh discipline policies and inadequate support services. These policies and practices disproportionately impact students of color, students with disabilities, and students from low-income families. Some of the key factors contributing to the school-to-prison pipeline include zero-tolerance discipline policies, the overuse of suspension and expulsion, the misuse of resource officers and police in schools, alongside a lack of access to mental health and other support services. Efforts to address the school-to-prison pipeline typically focus on reducing the use of harsh discipline, increasing access to support services, and improving relationships between schools and law enforcement. Those efforts to mitigate the problem are often unsuccessful and I will share with you why.

**Poverty and policing are closely linked.**

Low-income communities often experience higher levels of policing and police enforcement. Results include individuals living in poverty being disproportionately impacted by the criminal justice system. Police are often called upon to respond to issues such as homelessness, drug use, and mental health crises, which are often the result of a lack of resources and support. This can lead to over-policing of low-income communities, where police officers become more likely to make arrests, issue citations, and use force than in other areas. Additionally, low-income communities tend to have fewer resources such as private security, which can lead to more reliance on police to address sociological issues, not just crime. This in turn, perpetuates a cycle of over-policing and over-reliance on the criminal justice system to address social issues.

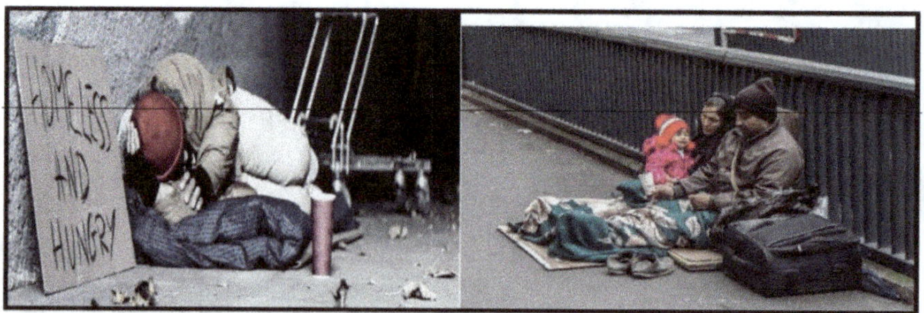



**Low-income communities also tend to have fewer resources to fight back against police misconduct, which can lead to a feeling of powerlessness and distrust of the police.**

To deal with the link between poverty and policing, efforts should be made to reduce over-policing of low-income communities, and an increase in community-based policing. Comprehensive safety, mental health, and job services designed to build trust and positive relationships between the police and the community, must be implemented. Additionally, providing resources and support to low-income communities, such as education, job training, and social services can help to address the underlying issues that contribute to poverty, reduce crime, and improve community-police relations. Furthermore, promoting policies and practices that increase police accountability, training in bias reduction, and cultural competency can also help to reduce the negative impact of policing on low-income communities.

Low-income communities are often plagued by neighborhood gangs. In most instances, they consist of groups of individuals who come together for protection, camaraderie, and or profit—often in a specific geographic area. These gangs can have a significant impact on the communities in which they operate and are often associated with criminal activity such as drug trafficking, extortion, and violence. Gangs can also have a negative impact on the individuals who are involved in them, leading to a cycle of poverty, incarceration, and social marginalization. Efforts to remedy gang activity typically focus on law enforcement strategies, such as increased policing and prosecution of gang members, as well as community-based interventions, such as providing education, job training, and other resources to at-risk youth, and violence prevention and reduction programs. Gangs can have a significant impact on schools and their surrounding communities, leading to increased violence, drug activity, and other criminal behavior. Schools located in areas with high levels of gang activity may experience higher rates of absenteeism, disciplinary problems, and lower academic achievement. Gangs often recruit new members from among the youth in schools and neighborhoods, which can lead to further involvement in criminal activity. To address the impact of gangs on our youth, schools and communities have implemented several strategies. One is to implement school-based programs that provide education, job training, and other resources to at-risk youth, which can provide an alternative to gang involvement. Another is to develop partnerships between schools, law enforcement agencies, and community organizations to address gang activity and provide support for at-risk youth. Additionally, schools can also adopt policies and practices that promote positive youth development, such as positive behavior support, restorative justice, and counseling services. Overall, addressing gangs in schools requires a comprehensive and multi-faceted approach that includes addressing the underlying issues that contribute to gang involvement, such as poverty and lack of opportunities, as well as providing support and alternatives for at-risk youth.

Poverty and incarceration are closely linked, as individuals living in poverty are more likely to be incarcerated than those with higher socioeconomic status. This is due to a variety of factors, including a lack of access to education, jobs, and other resources, which can lead to higher rates of crime and poverty. The problem is exacerbated by the criminal justice system disproportionately policing, arresting and imprisoning people from low-income communities. Individuals living in poverty are more likely to be affected by the high costs associated with the criminal justice system, such as bail, fines, and fees, which can fuel the cycle of poverty and incarceration. This cycle can be hard to break, as incarceration can make it even more difficult for individuals to find employment, housing, and other resources, leading to further poverty and recidivism.

To address the relationship between poverty and incarceration, efforts should be made to reduce the use of fines and fees, while providing alternatives to incarceration for individuals who are unable to pay them. Ultimately, there should be increased access to resources for low-income individuals and communities. This can include providing job training, education, and other reentry services to individuals while they are in prison, and providing targeted support such as housing and healthcare once they are released. Additionally, addressing poverty requires reducing poverty through increased access to education, jobs and other resources, as well as reducing over-policing, promoting community-based policing, and reforming the criminal justice system.

Poverty jail refers to the phenomenon that occurs when individuals are unable to pay fines or fees, often related to minor offenses resulting in jail time. This can lead to a cycle of poverty and incarceration, as the individual may lose their job or housing as a result of their incarceration. That loss of resources and stability makes it even more difficult for them to pay the fines or fees when they are released. This fact disproportionately affects low-income individuals and communities of color, who are more likely to be targeted by law enforcement. They are also most likely to have limited access to resources to pay fines or fees. Efforts to mitigate this financial hardship typically focuses on reducing fines and fees and providing alternatives to incarceration for individuals who are unable to pay.

Neighborhoods with high levels of poverty and low levels of economic opportunity are often disproportionately affected by mass incarceration and the criminal justice system. These areas are often characterized by a lack of access to education, jobs, and other resources, which can lead to high rates of crime and poverty. The criminal justice system then disproportionately polices, arrests, and imprisons residents of these neighborhoods, perpetuating the cycle of poverty and incarceration. This phenomenon is commonly referred to as the "neighborhoods to prison pipeline", which is similar to the "school-to-prison pipeline", but the former happens at the community level. Efforts to address the neighborhoods-to-prison pipeline typically focus on reducing poverty and increasing access to resources, such as education, jobs, and affordable housing, as well as reducing over-policing, promoting community-based policing, and reforming the criminal justice system. Poverty is one of the main factors that can contribute to the formation and spread of gangs in communities. Individuals living in poverty are often more vulnerable to the allure of gangs, which can offer a sense of belonging, protection, and economic opportunities that they may not have access to otherwise.

Poverty is a major barrier to educational attainment and success as shown using Maslow's (1943) hierarchy of needs. Children living in poverty are more likely to attend under-resourced schools, have less access to high-quality early childhood education, and are less likely to graduate from high school than their more affluent peers. One of the main ways poverty affects education is through a lack of access to resources. Children living in poverty are more likely to attend schools that lack basic resources such as textbooks, technology, and qualified teachers. They also have less access to extracurricular activities, such as sports and music programs, which can be important for their overall development and engagement in school.

Poverty can also affect children's health, nutrition, and stability which can impact their ability to attend school and learn. Children living in poverty are more likely to experience chronic stress, hunger, and poor health, which can lead to increased absenteeism and difficulty in concentration, negatively affecting their academic performance.

Addressing the link between poverty and education requires a multifaceted approach. This can include providing targeted resources and support to schools in low-income areas, increasing access to high-quality early childhood education, and providing families with financial assistance and social services, such as housing and healthcare. Additionally, implementing programs aimed at reducing poverty such as job training, and affordable housing can also help to improve educational outcomes for children living in poverty.

Privation and unemployment are closely connected, and one of the main reasons people fall into poverty is a lack of access to stable, well-paying jobs. People living in poverty are more likely to have limited education and job skills, which can make it difficult for them to find and maintain employment. Additionally, people living in poverty are more likely to live in areas with high unemployment rates, which can further limit their job opportunities.

Poverty can also make it difficult for individuals to meet the requirements of many jobs, such as reliable transportation and childcare, or to afford the costs associated with finding and keeping a job, such as professional clothing or a phone.

To address the link between poverty and unemployment, efforts must be made to create more jobs and job training programs, especially in disadvantaged communities. This can include government-funded job training programs, tax incentives for businesses that create jobs in low-income areas, and public works projects. Additionally, providing targeted financial assistance and social services, such as affordable housing and childcare, can help low-income individuals meet the basic requirements of employment and maintain stable jobs. Furthermore, addressing poverty also requires addressing broader economic policies that can lead to joblessness, such as lack of economic mobility, low wages, inequality, as well as providing policies that ensure fair and equal opportunities and access to jobs, such as anti-discrimination policies, and affordable education and training opportunities.

One of the most overlooked aspects of poverty is the lack of political representation. Individuals living in poverty often experience a lack of political representation and influence. This can be due to a variety of factors, such as a lack of access to information and resources. Other factors are limited political engagement and participation, and a lack of representation of low-income individuals and communities in government and politics. Individuals living with impoverished backgrounds are less likely to be registered to vote, less likely to vote, and less likely to have their voices heard in the political process. This can be due to a variety of reasons, such as lack of access to information, lack of transportation, and the challenges of balancing work and family responsibilities with the time and energy required to participate in politics. Additionally, low-income communities are less likely to have political representation in government, as they tend to have fewer resources to invest in political campaigns and lobbying efforts. To address the link between poverty and political representation, efforts should be made to increase political engagement and participation among low-income individuals and communities. Some issues may be remedied by increasing access to information, providing transportation and childcare assistance, and reducing barriers to voting. Additionally, providing resources and support to low-income individuals and communities, such as education, job training, and social services, can help address the underlying issues that contribute to poverty in hopes of reducing poverty and promoting political representation. Furthermore, promoting policies and practices that increase the representation of low-income individuals and communities in government and politics, such as public funding for political campaigns, redistricting reform, and fair representation can also help to increase the political representation of low-income communities.

Robert Merton's strain theory suggests that crime results from the strain or pressure experienced by individuals who are unable to achieve their goals through socially acceptable means. He argued that the unequal distribution of wealth and opportunity in society creates a gap between aspirations and the means to achieve them, leading some individuals to turn to crime. Merton's theory suggests that crime is not a result of individual deviance, but rather a response to societal structural factors.

Anomie refers to a state of social disorder or a breakdown in the norms and values that govern behavior in a society. It was first introduced by sociologist Emile Durkheim as a concept to describe the loss of direction and confusion that occurs when there is a disconnection between an individual's values and the values of the larger society. The term is often used to describe a situation in which the rules and regulations that govern behavior are unclear, or in which the norms and values that provide structure and meaning to social life are breaking down. In these circumstances, individuals may experience feelings of aimlessness, confusion, and a sense of disconnection from society.

The disconnection and confusion are constantly reinforced in minority communities by a justice system that is not just. A prime example is the murder of a 15-year-old Latasha Harlins by a Korean store owner.

Jae Jones (2022) writes "Latasha Harlins was a 15-year-old girl who was shot and killed on March 16, 1991 by Soon Ja Du, a 51-year-old Korean store owner. Harlins was a student at Westchester

High School in Los Angeles, California. Her death happened thirteen days after the videotape of the Rodney King beating was released. Store owner, Du, saw Harlins putting a bottle of orange juice in her backpack. She thought that the young girl was attempting to steal the bottle of juice, she did not see the money that Harlins had in her hand to pay for the juice. Du grabbed at Harlins by the sweater in an attempt to snatch her backpack, but Harlins struck Du three times with her fist, allegedly knocking her to the ground. After Harlins backed away from Du, Du picked up a stool and threw it at her. Harlins then picked up the orange juice that dropped during the scuffle and threw it on the counter and turned to leave the store. That is when Du reached under the counter to retrieve a handgun. She then fired at 15-year-old Harlins from behind at a distance of about three feet, shot her in the back of her head, killing her instantly. On November 15, 1991, the jury found Du guilty of voluntary manslaughter with a 16-year prison sentence recommendation, believing that Du's shooting was fully within her control, and she fired the gun voluntarily. The presiding judge, Joyce Karlin reduced the sentence to probation of five years, four hundred hours of community service, and a $500.00 fine" (para. 1-4).

When a 15-year-old girl is murdered and the killer serves not one day of jail time, it reinforces to the community that their lives do not matter and the justice system will not establish a social contract to serve minorities. This lack of value for Black, Native American, and Brown lives helps to fuel the application of Cooley's theory of the looking glass self, and its damaging effects.

The "looking-glass self" is a concept introduced by American sociologist Charles Horton Cooley. It refers to the idea that a person's self-concept is shaped by their perceived reflections in the attitudes and judgments of others. Cooley (1902) believed that people form their self-image based on how they imagine others see them, and that this perception influences their behavior and interactions with others. In this way, the self is not just a product of an individual's own thoughts and experiences but is also shaped by social relationships and the feedback that people receive from others.

Respect for all cultures is the first step on the road to uniting this country. The chains of generational poverty must be broken. This can only be accomplished by establishing a valid social contract with all who live in poverty. As we move further into the Fourth Industrial Revolution, the very fabric of American economics, education, and daily life will change. We as citizens must band together to ensure that the changes benefit all, not just the wealthy.

# Chapter 8

# Culture

**Culture is any aspect of social life.**

Culture in sociology refers to the shared beliefs, values, customs, behaviors, and artifacts that characterize a group or society. It encompasses all aspects of social life, including language, religion, social norms, material objects, and institutions. Culture is transmitted from one generation to the next, and helps to shape individual identities and social behaviors.

Those who suffer from generational poverty have developed cultural norms that most in mainstream America do not understand. The mores followed in many instances are necessary for survival. If law enforcement is to establish a just social contract with all citizens, it is imperative that they understand and respect all cultures within society. In many impoverished communities, distrust of the police forces individuals to handle problems in their own ways. This distrust is not unfounded or unearned, as minorities have been brutalized by bad actors wearing uniforms since the advent of police in this country. Lack of resources available to those living in poverty means no solving disputes in courts, which often leads to violent confrontations. Those who seek to involve the police in stamping out crime in their neighborhoods put their lives and the lives of loved ones at risk. It is difficult to understand from the outside looking in when it comes to the "no snitching" rule, yet that dynamic which benefits predators is real. There is a price to be paid by those who are viewed in the community as friendly to the police.

As a young lad, one of the first things I learned was to mind my own business. If I observed something untoward occurring, I was taught to leave the area, come home and report to my parents what I saw. Most importantly, I was not to interact with law enforcement. During the 1960's, Rochester, NY was policed by a department that visited violence upon minorities with impunity. It did not matter to them if a minority was guilty or innocent. When investigating a crime and interviewing a minority, they were known to beat people into confessing so they could say they solved the crime, even when they knew the person was innocent. They were proficient in the illegal methods that they used, to the point that in some instances, they left no physical indication of what they had done. One method that was truly dreaded involved the interrogator placing a phone book on the head of his victim and having his partner repeatedly strike the phone book with his nightstick. Understanding what we now know about brain damage and concussions, it makes one wonder about how many people were permanently damaged by the torturous practice.

The conscious and unconscious bias exhibited by law enforcement officers was off the charts. There were some outside basketball courts kids and I often used in the summer, on Webster Avenue of my hometown, Rochester, NY. One day, several of my friends and I were leaving the courts and an officer who patrolled the area was standing by the gate. He stopped us and began talking. He stated that he knew why we always wore tennis shoes. He then went on to say that it helped us to be quiet when we committed burglaries and to run from the police. It seemed that he was oblivious to the fact that playing ball in basketball shoes was the norm.

To understand the power of law enforcement in maintaining an unfair political system, one needs to understand the use of social control resources. Social control resources refer to the tools and strategies that individuals, organizations, and society use to regulate and influence behavior and attitudes. These resources can take many forms, including:

1. Norms and values: Shared cultural norms and values provide guidance on what is considered acceptable behavior and can be a source of social control.
2. Institutions: Institutions, such as schools, churches, and the criminal justice system, are often used as a means of social control.
3. Laws and regulations: Governments use laws and regulations to restrict certain behaviors and provide penalties for those who violate them.
4. Economic incentives and sanctions: Economic incentives and sanctions, such as rewards or punishments, can be used to influence behavior.
5. Social sanctions: Social sanctions, such as shame, stigma, or ostracism, can be used to discourage certain behaviors and reinforce social norms.
6. Mass media: The media can be used to shape public opinion, reinforce cultural norms, and influence behavior.

While social control resources can play an important role in maintaining social order and stability, they can also have negative effects, such as limiting individual freedom and reinforcing oppressive systems of power and control. It is important to consider the effects and consequences of different social control resources and to use them in ways that are ethical, fair, and respectful of individual rights and freedoms. In order to better understand, we must recognize the dynamics of integrating various cultures in our society.

The Melting Pot is a term used to describe a society where different cultural groups come together and blend to create a new unified culture. This concept originated in America and was used to describe the idea that immigrants from diverse backgrounds could come to the US, assimilate, and create a unique American culture. The melting pot concept suggests that different cultural groups blend their traditions, customs, and values to create a new, blended culture. This term is often used as a metaphor for cultural integration and diversity in a society. However, it has been criticized for implying that all cultures must give up their unique characteristics to create a homogeneous society, and for ignoring the ongoing presence of distinct cultural groups. The melting pot was a viable concept early on in American history when immigration primarily consisted of Europeans. Yet, as other cultures of the world, who were readily identifiable by their skin color began to immigrate to the U.S., the melting pot was found not to be a viable paradigm for all. Another concept more sensitive to cultures' various norms and mores was needed. This resulted in a move from the melting pot to the salad bowl view of assimilation.

The salad bowl is a term used to describe a society where different cultural groups coexist, but maintain their unique traditions, customs, and values, rather than blending into a single, unified culture. The salad bowl concept suggests that cultural groups in a society can maintain their distinctiveness while also coexisting and interacting with one another. This term is often used as a metaphor for cultural diversity and pluralism in a society. Unlike the melting pot concept, which implies that all cultures must blend together, the salad bowl concept emphasizes the importance of preserving cultural differences and recognizes the value of a diverse, multicultural society. It is vitally important that this salad be represented in all aspects of society. Although the salad bowl, if applied correctly, will make America stronger than it has ever been, there are those who want to keep us divided by misrepresenting the concept and causing fear and resentment in certain segments of the population. The in vogue scare tactic most currently promulgated is the great replacement theory.

"The Great Replacement Theory" and "The Salad Bowl" are two different concepts that offer vastly different views of cultural diversity. The Great Replacement Theory is a conspiracy theory that suggests that there is a deliberate plot to replace the white European population with non-white people through mass migration and low birth rates among white Europeans. This theory has been widely debunked by scholars and experts in the field of demography, who argue that it is based on flawed data and false assumptions.

On the other hand, "The Salad Bowl" is a metaphor used to describe the way in which different cultures can coexist within a society without losing their unique identities. In a salad bowl, each ingredient retains its distinctive flavor and texture while contributing to the overall flavor of the dish. Similarly, in a multicultural society, each culture can maintain its unique traditions and practices while contributing to the richness of the broader culture. Overall, the Great Replacement Theory is a harmful and baseless conspiracy theory that has been discredited by experts, while the Salad Bowl is a more positive and inclusive metaphor that promotes the idea of cultural diversity and coexistence.

Exploring the pros and cons of a multicultural society proves that the benefits far outweigh the drawbacks. It also indicates that the negatives can be mitigated if society deems it important. A multicultural society is a community in which people from different ethnic, racial, and cultural backgrounds live together. Here are some potential pros and cons of a multicultural society:

**Pros:**
1. Diversity: A multicultural society celebrates diversity and creates an opportunity for people to learn about different cultures and traditions.
2. Cultural exchange: People from different cultural backgrounds can share their unique skills and knowledge, leading to the exchange of ideas and new ways of thinking.
3. Economic growth: A multicultural society can lead to economic growth through the creation of new businesses, the promotion of tourism, and the development of new trade relationships.
4. Creativity: Exposure to different perspectives and cultures can inspire creativity and innovation.

**Cons:**

1. Social tension: A multicultural society can create social tension, especially if there are cultural clashes and misunderstandings between different groups.
2. Isolation: It is possible for people to isolate themselves within their own cultural groups, leading to a lack of interaction and understanding between different cultures.
3. Discrimination: Prejudice and discrimination can occur when people from different cultural backgrounds are not treated equally, leading to inequality and injustice.
4. Language barriers: In a multicultural society, language can be a significant barrier to communication and integration, making it difficult for people to work and live together effectively.

Overall, a multicultural society can have both advantages and disadvantages. It is important to recognize and address the challenges that may arise, and work towards promoting mutual understanding and respect between different cultural groups.

As a high school student in the 1970's, I remember being introduced to the country of India as part of the social studies curriculum. Much despair was felt for the lower caste in Indian society, as I learned of the inequities suffered through no fault of their own. What was not taught and what I was too young to understand is the fact that Native American, Brown, and Black cultures exist in the same system here in America.

Class and caste struggle refers to the ongoing social, economic, and political conflict between different groups in society based on their socioeconomic status and caste or ethnic background. Class struggle refers to the conflict between social classes, such as the working class and the upper class, over resources, power, and wealth. This conflict often takes place within the economic and political systems, as different classes compete for control over resources and decision-making power. Caste struggle, on the other hand, refers to the conflict between different castes in societies that have a caste system, such as India. This conflict often stems from the unequal distribution of power and resources between castes, and the entrenched social hierarchy that reinforces caste-based discrimination.

Both class and caste struggles can have significant impacts on individuals' lives, and on society as a whole. These conflicts can contribute to social tensions and inequality, as well as to political and economic instability. Efforts to address class and caste struggles often involve advocating for social and economic equality, challenging the existing power structures, and promoting the rights and well-being of marginalized groups. Our current law enforcement system is designed to protect the status quo, which is not an effective social contract for the majority of Americans. Those citizens are then scapegoated and assigned the label of counterculture, while being blamed for most societal issues.

Counterculture refers to a cultural movement or subculture that opposes or rejects the dominant cultural norms and values of society. It is often characterized by non-conformity, anti-establishment views, and alternative lifestyles and beliefs. Countercultural movements can emerge in response to political, social, or economic issues and can challenge the status quo in various ways, whether that be through art, music, fashion, or political activism. Examples of countercultures include the hippie movement of the 1960s, the punk movement of the 1970s, and various youth subcultures that have arisen in response to mainstream culture. Minorities who advocate for equal rights are viewed as counterculture as they struggle to attain a valid social contract.

**"Police culture refers to the shared values, beliefs, attitudes, behaviors, and practices that exist within a police organization or law enforcement agency."**

The issues between police and minorities is exacerbated by the fact that law enforcement, as an institution, is designed to make citizens conform to the values of those in power, regardless of the equity or truth in actions. Police culture refers to the shared values, beliefs, attitudes, behaviors, and practices that exist within a police organization or law enforcement agency. It encompasses both formal and informal aspects of policing, and often involves a strong emphasis on loyalty, obedience, and a "law and order" mentality. Police culture can influence the actions and decisions of individual officers and shape the overall behavior of the agency. Some elements of police culture can also contribute to negative outcomes, such as excessive use of force and a lack of accountability.

The most effective tool in fighting racism, oppression, and inequity is common unity of all citizens. Common unity and community are keys to change for the betterment of the majority of our society. Common unity refers to a shared sense of community, belonging, and purpose among a group of people. It involves a recognition of the common experiences, values, and goals that connect individuals and creates a sense of solidarity. Common unity can be found within a variety of groups, including families, communities, religious organizations, and political movements.

Having a sense of common unity can bring people together, increase social cohesion, and foster a sense of belonging. It can also lead to increased collaboration and cooperation, as individuals work together towards shared goals. However, the development of common unity is not always automatic or easy and can require effort and compromise from all parties involved. For example, differences in beliefs, values, or experiences can create divisions and challenges to creating a sense of common unity. It can also be difficult to maintain common unity over time, as new challenges and changes can test the strength of the groups' bonds. Overall, common unity is seen as a key factor in creating a strong, cohesive, and functional community, and is often an important goal in efforts to promote social and political change.

Most damaging to common unity is social projection. Social projection refers to the process by which individuals attribute their own thoughts, feelings, and attitudes to other people or groups. This means that individuals tend to assume that others have similar thoughts, feelings, and attitudes to their own. Social projection can result in stereotypes, generalizations, and misunderstandings. For example, if someone is feeling angry, they might assume that others around them are also feeling angry, even if there is no evidence to support this assumption. They might also project their own anger onto others, interpreting the actions of others as angry or hostile even if this is not the case. Social projection is a common phenomenon and can be influenced by various factors, such as prior experiences, cultural background, and cognitive biases. It can also be influenced by the way information is presented, such as the way events are portrayed in the media, or the way individuals describe their experiences.

Overall, social projection can have important impacts on social interactions and relationships, as it can lead to misunderstandings, conflicts, and prejudice. It is important to be aware of social projection and to take steps to avoid projecting one's own thoughts, feelings, and attitudes onto others. This can involve being open to different perspectives, considering alternative explanations for the behavior of others, and being mindful of the ways in which one's own biases and experiences can influence perceptions. It is social projection that is used by certain politicians to keep cultures separated and warring with each other, while those in power fleece the country unimpeded by those most affected.

# References


Benson, E. (2003). *Rehabilitate or punish?*. Monitor on Psychology. https://www.apa.org/monitor/julaug03/rehab.html#:~:text=But%20in%20the%201980s%2C%20many,U.S.%20Department%20of%20Justice%20estimates.

Blakemore, E. (2021, February 8). *Reconstruction offered a glimpse of equality for Black Americans. Why did it fail?*. History. https://www.nationalgeographic.com/history/article/reconstruction-turbulent-post-civil-war-period-explained

Browne, J. (2007). *Rooted in slavery: Prison labor exploitation*. Reimagine. https://www.reimaginerpe.org/node/856

Carr, N. (2021, February 1). *New video surfaces of racist exchange between former Georgia police chief, officer*. WSB. https://www.wsbtv.com/news/local/new-video-surfaces-racist-exchange-between-former-georgia-police-chief-officer/V7KN5DMGIZDEDKFS6KYSNEWX64/

Carroll, H. (2016, September). *Serious mental illness prevalence in jails and Prisons*. Treatment Advocacy Center. https://www.treatmentadvocacycenter.org/evidence-and-research/learn-more-about/3695

Chandler, D. L. (2021, August 25). *Abner Louima was savagely beaten by NYPD 24 Years Ago Today*. NewsOne. https://newsone.com/2029939/abner-louima-case/

Cherry, K. (2022, November 12). *The psychology behind why we strive for Consensus*. Verywell Mind. https://www.verywellmind.com/what-is-groupthink-2795213

Cole, N. L. (2019, February 12). *How Michel Foucalt influenced the field of sociology*. ThoughtCo. https://www.thoughtco.com/michel-foucault-biography-3026478

Collins, D., Thompson, C., Balsamo, M., & Wawrow, J. (2022, June 1). *10 dead in Buffalo Supermarket Attack Police Call Hate Crime*. AP News. https://apnews.com/article/buffalo-supermarket-shooting-442c6d97a073f39f99d006dbba40f64b

Confronting Violent White Supremacy Part IV: White Supremacy in Blue_The Infiltration of Local Police Department: Hearing before the U.S. House of Representative Subcommittee on Civil Rights and Civil Liberties, 116th Cong. (2020). https://www.govinfo.gov/content/pkg/CHRG-116hhrg41981/html/CHRG-116hhrg41981.htm

Crawford, K. (2015, October 10). *Review of deadly force incident: Tamir Rice - Cuyahoga County, Ohio*. Cuyahoga County Prosecutor. http://prosecutor.cuyahogacounty.us/pdf_prosecutor/en-US/Tamir%20Rice%20Investigation/Crawford-Review%20of%20Deadly%20Force-Tamir%20Rice.pdf

Daniels, R. (2019, December 5). *Prisons neglect pregnant women in their healthcare policies*. Prison Policy Initiative. https://www.prisonpolicy.org/blog/2019/12/05/pregnancy/

DeLong, W. (2021, November 29). *Frank Serpico uncovered NYPD corruption so startling, his own colleagues nearly let him die*. All That's Interesting. https://allthatsinteresting.com/frank-serpico

Durkee, A. (2022a, August 4). *Vast majority of Americans don't want abortion bans, poll finds-even in states where it's already outlawed*. Forbes. https://www.forbes.com/sites/alisondurkee/2022/08/02/vast-majority-of-americans-dont-want-abortion-bans-poll-finds-even-in-states-where-its-already-outlawed/?sh=45018438795c

Durkee, A. (2022b, October 2). *100 days since Roe v. Wade was overturned: The 11 biggest consequences*. Forbes. https://www.forbes.com/sites/alisondurkee/2022/10/02/100-days-since-roe-v-wade-was-overturned-the-11-biggest-consequences/

Ellis, A. (2016, July 25). *Securing a favorable federal prison placement*. Alan Ellis Attorney. https://alanellis.com/securing-favorable-federal-prison-placement/#:~:text=The%20Federal%20Prison%20System,risk%20of%20violence%20or%20escape.

Elwell, F. W. (n.d.). *Lenski's Evolutionary Theory*. Gerhard Lenski's ecological-evolutionary theory.
http://www.faculty.rsu.edu/users/f/felwell/www/Theorists/Essays/Lenski2.htm

Federal Bureau of Prisons. (2023, July 29). *Federal Bureau of Prisons*. BOP Statistics: Prison Security Levels.
https://www.bop.gov/about/statistics/statistics_inmate_sec_levels.jsp

Fertig, N. (2022, July 21). *Schumer's legal weed bill is finally here*. POLITICO.
https://www.politico.com/news/2022/07/21/schumer-legal-weed-bill-00047058

Galletta, E., Fagan, T. J., Shapiro, D., & Walker, L. E. (2021, March 18). *Societal reentry of prison inmates with mental illness: Obstacles ...* Journal of Correctional Health Care. https://www.liebertpub.com/doi/10.1089/jchc.19.04.0032

Gerhold, R. (2021, January 20). *Norway vs. US: How different are their prison systems?*. Kent Partnership. https://www.kentpartnership.org/what-norways-prison-system-can-teach-the-united-states/#:~:text=Halden%20is%20a%20maximum%2Dsecurity,similar%20to%20the%20general%20population.

Goodyear, D. (2022, May 30). *The L.A. County Sheriff's deputy-gang crisis*. The New Yorker. https://www.newyorker.com/magazine/2022/06/06/the-la-county-sheriffs-deputy-gang-crisis

Greenberg, D. (1994, August 10). *Term limits: The only way to clean up Congress*. The Heritage Foundation. https://www.heritage.org/political-process/report/term-limits-the-only-way-clean-congress

Hauptman, M. (2021, August 13). *"Warrior mindset" police training proliferated. then, high-profile deaths put it under scrutiny*. The Washington Post.
https://www.washingtonpost.com/nation/2021/08/11/police-training-warrior-mindset-killology/

Helms, R. (2009, January 26). *Modeling the politics of punishment: A conceptual and empirical analysis of "law in action" in criminal sentencing*. Journal of Criminal Justice.
https://www.sciencedirect.com/science/article/pii/S0047235208001384

Hyle, K. (2021, September 1). *The Federal Register*. FederalRegister.gov. https://www.federalregister.gov/documents/2021/09/01/2021-18800/annual-determination-of-average-cost-of-incarceration-fee-coif

Jones, J. (2022, July 10). *15-year-old Latasha Harlins killed over a bottle of orange juice*. Black Then. https://blackthen.com/15-year-old-latasha-harlins-killed-over-a-bottle-of-orange-juice/

Kanu, H. (2022, May 12). *Prevalence of white supremacists in law enforcement demands drastic change*. Reuters. https://www.reuters.com/legal/government/prevalence-white-supremacists-law-enforcement-demands-drastic-change-2022-05-12/

Lepore, J. (2020, July 13). *The invention of the police*. The New Yorker. https://www.newyorker.com/magazine/2020/07/20/the-invention-of-the-police

Levin, S. (2016, June 27). *Stanford trial judge overseeing much harsher sentence for similar assault case*. The Guardian. https://www.theguardian.com/us-news/2016/jun/27/stanford-sexual-assault-trial-judge-persky

Lubin, G., Kelley, M. B., & Wile, R. (2012, March 20). *Meet the 24 robber barons who once ruled America*. Business Insider. https://www.businessinsider.com/americas-robber-barons-2012-3

Mcleod, S. (2023, June 23). *Operant conditioning: What it is, how it works, and examples*. Simply Psychology. https://www.simplypsychology.org/operant-conditioning.html

Miles, F. (2020, February 12). *What happened to "affluenza" teen ethan couch? A history of a family breaking the law*. Fox News. https://www.foxnews.com/us/what-happened-affluenza-teen-ethan-couch

Modvig, J., (2014). Violence, sexual abuse and torture in prisons. In Møller, L., Galea, G., & Udesen, C. (Eds.), *Prisons and health* (pp. 19-26). World Health Organization. Retrieved from https://apps.who.int/iris/bitstream/handle/10665/128603/9789289050593-eng.pdf?sequence=3&isAllowed=y

Moffit, R. (1992, April 16). *Congress and the taxpayers: A double standard on health care reform?*. The Heritage Foundation. https://www.heritage.org/health-care-reform/report/congress-and-the-taxpayers-double-standard-health-care-reform

Moinzadeh, A. (2017, February 28). *Kalief Browder's life was stolen by the prison system. his sister remembers the boy she lost.* The FADER. https://www.thefader.com/2017/02/28/nicole-browder-kalief-browder-interview-prison-system

Murphy, P. (2020, September 29). *Both sides of the debate.* The Prison System Rehabilitation vs Punishment. https://blog.mcdaniel.edu/rehabvspun/2020/09/29/both-sides-of-the-debate/

NAACP. (2022, February 11). *History of lynching in America.* NAACP. https://naacp.org/find-resources/history-explained/history-lynching-america

NBCNews. (2014). *Police pay gap: Many of America's finest struggle on poverty wages.* NBCNews.com. https://www.nbcnews.com/feature/in-plain-sight/police-pay-gap-many-americas-finest-struggle-poverty-wages-n232701

Nellis, A. (2021, October 13). *The Color of Justice: Racial and ethnic disparity in state prisons.* The Sentencing Project. https://www.sentencingproject.org/reports/the-color-of-justice-racial-and-ethnic-disparity-in-state-prisons-the-sentencing-project/

Oliver, W. (1970, January 1). *August vollmer: The father of American policing.* Carolina Academic Press. https://cap-press.com/books/isbn/9781611635591/August-Vollmer

Onibada, A. (2021, July 22). *How the legacy of Sundown Towns Affects Black Travelers.* BuzzFeed News. https://www.buzzfeednews.com/article/adeonibada/sundown-towns-racism-black-drivers-tiktok

Origins and foundations of American Courts - McLean County, Illinois. (2011, June 15). https://mcleancountyil.gov/DocumentCenter/View/231/Foundations_and-organization_Illinois_Courts?bidId=

PBS. (n.d.). *Chain Gangs.* Slavery by Another Name. https://www.pbs.org/tpt/slavery-by-another-name/themes/chain-gangs/

Punsalan-Teigen, P. (2021, May 10). *Mississippi Black Codes, 1865-1866 .* BlackPast. https://www.blackpast.org/african-american-history/events-african-american-history/mississippi-black-codes-1865-1866/

Roth, A. (2020). *Insane: America's criminal treatment of mental illness.* Basic Books.

Sandoval, P., & Couwels, J. (2022, July 6). *Jayland Walker was handcuffed when his body arrived at the medical examiner's office, according to the autopsy report.* CNN. https://www.cnn.com/2022/07/05/us/jayland-walker-handcuffed-autopsy-report/index.html

Schwartz, K. (2020, November 19). *How a berkeley police chief gave rise to the Modern Force.* KQED. https://www.kqed.org/news/11847612/who-was-august-vollmer-and-is-he-responsible-for-the-modern-police-force

Serbin, S. (2019, February 5). *Inmate suffering eyesight loss after attack in Muscogee County Jail.* https://www.wtvm.com. https://www.wtvm.com/2019/02/05/inmate-left-with-eyesight-loss-after-attack-muscogee-county-jail/

Silverman, H. (2020, June 2). *Police officers are joining protesters for prayers and hugs in several US cities.* CNN. https://www.cnn.com/2020/06/02/us/police-protesters-together/index.html

*Sitting bull: "the warrior is not someone who fights."* Historical Snapshots. (2023, March 9). https://historicalsnaps.com/2018/08/19/sitting-bull-the-warrior-is-not-someone-who-fights/

Stoughton, S., Katz, W., Joh, E. E., & Karakatsanis, A. (2015, April 10). *Law enforcement's "warrior" problem.* Harvard Law Review. https://harvardlawreview.org/2015/04/law-enforcements-warrior-problem/

Subcommittee on Civil Rights and Civil Liberties, & Raskin, J. [Report], Confronting Violent White Supremacy Part IV: White Supremacy in Blue_The Infiltration of Local Police Departments (2020).

Thompson, C., Balsamo, M., & Collins, D. (2022, May 14). *Buffalo mass shooting: 10 dead, suspect arrested.* Police1. https://www.police1.com/active-shooter/articles/buffalo-mass-shooting-10-dead-suspect-arrested-DfSAa1Wbe4tdKoWK/

Tucker, E. (2022, July 10). *Why did Ohio officers Handcuff Jayland Walker after shooting him dozens of times?.* CNN. https://www.cnn.com/2022/07/09/us/jayland-walker-police-handcuffs/index.html

U.S Government Publishing Office. (2020). Confronting violent white supremacy (part IV): White supremacy in ... https://www.congress.gov/event/116th-congress/house-event/LC65641/text?s=1&r=1

Williams, C. (2018, December 17). *Sheriff: Multiple inmates stabbed recently in Muscogee County Jail*. WRBL. https://www.wrbl.com/news/local-news/sheriff-multiple-inmates-stabbed-recently-in-muscogee-county-jail/

Wise, D. (2019). *Federal Prison Security Levels*. Federal Prison Time. https://www.federalprisontime.com/federal-prison-security-levels

Worth, R. F. (1995, November 1). *A model prison*. The Atlantic. https://www.theatlantic.com/magazine/archive/1995/11/a-model-prison/308518/